RULES
ONE NIGHT SERIES
WE BREAK
DANA ISALY

RULES WE BREAK
Copyright © 2023 Dana Isaly
All rights reserved.
Published: Dana Isaly 2023

No parts of this book may be reproduced in any form without written consent from the author. Except in the use of brief quotations in a book review.
This book is a piece of fiction. Any names, characters, businesses, places or events are a product of the author's imagination or are used fictitiously. Any resemblance to persons living or dead, events or locations is purely coincidental.
This book is licensed for your personal enjoyment only. This book may not be resold or given away to other people. If you are reading this book and have not purchased it for your use only, then you should return it to your favorite book retailer and purchase your own copy.
Thank you for respecting the author's work.

Editing: Sandra at One Love Editing
Cover Design: Pink Elephant Designs
Formatting: Pink Elephant Designs

CONTENT WARNING

This book is intended for those over the age of legal adulthood. There are graphic sexual scenes that include spanking, toy play, and more of that nature. Fertility issues are discussed briefly.

To the women who like their men to beg...this one is for you.

PLAYLIST

All On My Mind by Anderson East
Body by Rosenfeld
Love is a Bitch by Two Feet
Chainsmoking by Jasob Banks
Down To Ride by Kodoku
Do It For Me by Rosenfeld
Movement by Hozier

PROLOGUE

Greg, a year ago in Tokyo

I run into the office building, fixing my tie as I enter the elevator. Fuck, she sounded pissed on the phone. Ivy has been one hell of a boss ever since I joined this department. She constantly rides my ass, making sure I'm given all of the extra tasks that no one else seems to be able to handle.

And while that's all well and good because I do, in fact, get paid an ample amount of overtime, it makes it so I barely have a life outside of work. When I heard she was going to be visiting the Tokyo offices at the same time I was, I knew I was in for a harder work vacation than I had originally planned.

I should be with my friends right now, taking them out to celebrate the new relationship and the others that are still growing and strong. We should be partying, living it up on this once-in-a-lifetime trip we were able to take together.

But no. I'm here. Waiting on my boss hand and fucking foot.

"Mr. Ellis!" I jump as the doors open. How the hell she timed my arrival so perfectly, I don't know. "Just in time. Follow me, please."

Her hair is pulled back in a severely tight bun today, and her dark blue dress is just as tight. I can't help but watch the way her ass sways in it as she walks. As we pass everyone in their cubicles, they viciously type or file or talk into their phones at double the speed.

They know that when she's here, they're to be on their best behavior, constantly working even when there might be no work to do. It's just the type of boss she is. Her reputation spread far, and it spread quickly when she was hired on last year.

And while she may be difficult to work for, every single change she made has taken the company that much further. Our profits have almost doubled, and our employee turnover is almost nonexistent.

I follow her into her office, and I close the door behind us. This office is left open specifically for her. It's a corner office with so much natural light it almost blinds you when you walk in. Two of her walls are just floor-to-ceiling windows.

"Close the blinds," she says as she walks around her desk. I do as she asks, effectively closing off her view into the office. While it makes me want to shit myself because now I'm alone with her, it also gives the employees a break from her laser-beam gaze.

Once all the blinds are closed, I take a seat in one of the leather chairs in front of her desk. I clear my throat and try to get comfortable, although I don't think there's any getting comfortable in her presence anymore.

Not after what happened.

And when she turns those harsh blue eyes on me, I swear to god I break out in a cold sweat.

Fuck, she's going to fire me. She's going to fire me, and I'm never going to be able to get another job again because if you're fired by Ivy fucking Wallace, you're untouchable in any city you try to escape to. She's the grim reaper of corporate America.

"Greg," she starts, her legs crossing and her eyes falling to the desk in front of her. "What happened with you a couple weeks ago..."

"It won't happen again," I say, cutting her off in a rush of words. "I swear. It will never happen again. From here on out, I am nothing if not the angel of the office. I will come in early and leave late. Everything is business one hundred percent of the time."

She looks at me again, her eyes piercing into my fucking soul. She looks...worried?

"That's what you want?" she asks.

Her question catches me off guard. What I want? What I want is most definitely not that. I don't want to come in early and leave late. I don't want more responsibility. I want less. Working for her is exhausting, and I feel like I'm constantly missing out on things because I have to be at the office instead of with the people I love.

"Because that's not what I want."

I sit there in silence, staring at her, waiting to see where she's going with this. There's no way she can be thinking what I think she's thinking. There's no way that she wants what happened to happen again. I almost laugh at the absurdity of it, but I catch myself at the last moment.

She stands up and walks around her desk, stopping when she's in front of me to lean back on it. She crosses her legs at her ankles, and her hands go back to the solid wood behind her. I hate that I notice it makes her breasts pop out just a little bit further from the neckline of her dress.

"My eyes are up here, Mr. Ellis."

I feel the color drain from my face as I quickly look up at her face. I didn't even realize I was staring. Christ, I need to get ahold of myself.

"Are you going to fire me?" I finally ask.

"Fire you?" Her voice is incredulous, like it's the last thing that was on her mind. Like she can't even comprehend why I'm asking her that. "Why would I fire you?"

She even laughs a little.

What the fuck is happening.

"I don't know, Ivy. Maybe because I bent you over your desk back in California and fucked you until you screamed my name?" The words are out of my mouth before I can stop them. "And not only that, but we've been sexting and having phone sex ever since? I figured we may be at a point where you thought that needed to stop."

"Do you want it to stop?" she asks, her voice dropping lower as she leans forward and rests her hands on the sides of my chair. It puts me right at eye level with her chest, and I can't help but look again. My cock is stirring in my pants, all the blood in my body rushing south as she bites her lip and smiles.

"I don't want it to stop," she continues. "Actually, I think I'd like to step it up a notch."

Slowly, she puts one knee on one side of my thighs and then the other until her warm center is pressed against the crotch of my pants. She runs her hands through my hair and roughly pulls on it, forcing my head up to look at her.

"I think I'd like you to fuck me again." She kisses me. "And again." She bites my lip. "And again," she whispers.

My hands go to her hips, and I squeeze them hard, pulling her tighter against me. Her hips move, grinding against my own and giving my now very hard cock the attention it wants. She moans into my mouth, and I let my hands roam her body, moving up and over her waist until they reach her tits. My thumbs graze her nipples, and she sighs into me, holding my face tightly against hers.

"I don't know how good of an idea this is," I tell her when she lets me come up for air. "What if someone finds out? What if we get caught?"

"We'll just have to be smart about it," she says with a smile. A smile that speaks all kinds of promises. "No fucking in the office unless it's empty. No meeting out in public." She kisses me. "No messages through the work chat or email."

She kisses me again, harder this time. It feels like she's sucking my soul from my body, and I'm too happy to let her. Our tongues play together, and our teeth clash while her hips continue to rub against me.

"Okay." I take a deep breath when she finally peels herself off me. "Okay, yeah. Sounds great."

I can hear myself sounding like a fucking idiot. But she does that to me. When I'm in her presence, I go from my normal, confident, emotionless self to a teenage boy just waiting to do whatever she tells me to do.

"Good." She smiles and climbs off my lap, adjusting her dress back into place and smoothing out her hair. Walking back around her desk, she sits back in her chair and begins typing.

I sit there for a moment, not sure what I'm supposed to do now. And after a couple of minutes, she looks back to me like she's surprised I'm still here.

"You can go now, Greg," she says. "I expect the Harlowe account on my desk within the hour."

"I—uh, okay. Yes, ma'am," I stutter as I stand and tuck my raging boner into my waistband. She laughs softly as she watches me get my flustered self together. When I go to open her office door and leave, she stops me one last time.

"And I expect you at my place tonight," she tells me, typing again on her computer. "Midnight."

I nod and leave the room.

What the fuck just happened?

1

One year later...

My ass is dragging.

I was supposed to catch an evening flight out of LAX last night, but because there were storms in Nashville, I wasn't able to board until after midnight. That means that I have been awake for over twenty-four hours, and while I would love to go straight up to my room and go to sleep, I can't. I have fucking meetings to attend.

Grabbing an Uber from BNA, I quickly tell them I'm taking a power nap and slink down into my seat. I cover my eyes and pray for sleep, but the constant jostling of the car keeps me away and almost makes me nauseated. So much for that idea.

"We're here," she says as we pull up to the Four Seasons. "Sorry if that traffic kept you awake. It's always busy here anymore."

I try to smile politely as I thank her, but I'm not sure how kind the gesture looked. I haven't seen myself in a mirror yet, but I know I must look rough. I didn't have time for a haircut before I left, meaning my hair is longer than it normally is. That paired with dark circles from no sleep and wrinkly clothes from too long in an airport...I'm sure I look a fucking wreck.

It'll be a miracle if the Four Seasons doesn't run me away from scaring all the other wealthy guests.

My check-in was last night, so thankfully, it doesn't matter that I'm showing up here at—I check the time—Christ, it's 7:00 a.m. I have all of thirty minutes before the first meeting starts. Thank god it's in this hotel. Should give me enough time to shower.

"Greg Ellis," I tell the young lady at the front desk. "I was supposed to check in last night, but the storms delayed the flight."

She gives me a sympathetic smile.

"So sorry about that, Mr. Ellis. Luckily, you are staying in the Four Seasons." She leans forward like she's sharing a secret. "The best rooms, the most comfortable beds, and phenomenal room service. You'll be feeling better in no time."

Didn't say I felt bad, so that confirms my suspicions that I look bad.

I nod and give her another one of my polite smiles.

"Thank you."

She hands me the key card, and after I tell her I won't need help with my bags, she points me in the direction of my elevator.

As I start to walk away, thankful I still have twenty-three minutes before the meeting, I hear Ivy's silky voice call out my name. I've had minimal interactions with her over the past ten months, and truth be told, I kind of forgot there would be a lot of time spent with her in crowded rooms this weekend.

Ivy Wallace. My boss. My boss that I fucked...a lot.

It's been a year since Tokyo, where we decided we were going to explore whatever it was we had between us. It lasted all of two months before we both decided to put a stop to it. The anxiety I was experiencing on a daily basis was all-consuming. I couldn't sleep, wondering if we would be found out and I would lose my job. The thought of losing my job due to a situation like that was enough to give me panic attacks. I would be untouchable in the rest of the corporate world.

And she was just as worried, not wanting any of her colleagues to find out. It never looks good when a woman in power is fucking a subordinate. Or any employee for that matter. When a man does it? Hell yeah, roll out the red carpet and champagne. But for her, it could have been reputation destroying. She would never be taken seriously again.

So we stopped after two months of amazing, mind-blowing sex. She's a little dominant in the bedroom, and I fucking love that. Just thinking about it now makes my tired dick twitch in my pants. We were great together—our chemistry was off the charts. Ever since, we've been avoiding each other as much as possible. We are cordial in the halls if we pass one another, but I've been put on cases that she doesn't oversee, and even my office was moved onto a different floor.

"Greg!" she says again, and I can hear the smile in her voice. It's a change from her stern office voice.

I run my hands through my hair as I turn around, embarrassed that this is how she's going to see me for the first time in a while. But I get distracted when I face her because she is breathtaking. Her straight hair is down, lying over her shoulders and chest. She's dyed it since I last saw her, and now it's almost black. Fuck if it doesn't make her damn blue eyes pop even more.

She's dressed in a stylish, olive-green pantsuit that flatters her small waist and long legs. The arms of her jacket are rolled up, exposing the little tattoo she has on her wrist. With the heels she's wearing, she almost reaches my height.

"Hi, Ms. Walsh." I've reverted back to professionalism, not wanting to seem too close to her if anyone is within earshot.

"You look exhausted." She makes a face, and I don't miss the way her hand begins to reach out to me before she thinks better of it. Instead, she crosses them beneath her breasts.

"Flight was canceled because of the storms," I explain. "I literally just walked through the door."

"Skip the first meeting. Get some sleep."

I can't help myself—I raise an eyebrow and smirk in her direction. I've rarely seen this side of her in public. Normally, she saves the softer side of her for the bedroom when she's had her fill of orgasms and a full night's sleep.

"Oh, Gregory," she says with a delicate laugh. Her hand finally reaches out and touches my bicep. "Don't look at me like that." Her hand squeezes it. "You look like shit. Go up to your room, take a shower, and have a fucking nap. You're not going to be good to anyone in that state."

I sigh, knowing she's right. My brain is mush, and my limbs are struggling to hold me up. I used to be able to work like this all the time, wired on caffeine. But I'm getting older. Shit, I turned thirty this year, and suddenly, my joints are sore every day, and one cup of coffee doesn't do what it used to. But one glass of alcohol? I have heartburn and a headache the next day. My body is slowly starting to betray me.

"Yeah, fine. Okay." I sigh. "I do feel like shit."

She smiles and pulls her hand back to her person.

"I'd like to have a chat with you this weekend...catch up." She looks unsure of herself. I don't know who this woman is because she doesn't look anything like the bossy woman I knew when we first started fucking around. "Would that be okay?"

Those sapphire eyes look up at me from under dark eyelashes, and the longer I stare, the pinker her cheeks go.

"Yeah, of course," I finally answer. "It's been a while, hasn't it?"

"It has," she agrees, nodding. Her confidence slips back into place. "Next meeting is at one. I assume you'll be ready to go by then?"

I give her a little salute, and my ego swells a bit when she laughs quietly. I always loved that I was able to make her laugh when no one else around the office did.

"Get some sleep," she says, turning on her heel to walk back toward where I assume one of the conference rooms is. "You look like shit," she tosses over her shoulder with a smirk.

I shamelessly watch her ass sway while she walks away. Her heels are clicking on the tile floor, and her dark hair softly moves with each step. God, I miss wrapping it in my fist as I fuck her from behind, her tight ass rippling with each thrust inside of her.

When she's out of eyesight, I give myself a mental shake and try to catch my bearings. Finding the direction I was previously heading in, I see the elevator and make aim for it. And of course, the thing is filled with mirrors, giving me a lovely 360 view of my trashed-looking self.

"Jesus Christ," I murmur as I run my hands through my hair and over my face. "You look like shit, bro."

When I close my eyes, all I see is Ivy's ass and playful smirk. Even though I'm exhausted, my cock comes to life with the memories. I wonder what the hell she wants to talk about tonight. My dick is thrilled, hoping she wants to go another round, even if it's only for the one night.

It throbs as the elevator doors open. My room is a quick walk down the hall, and I've resigned myself to rubbing one out in the shower. After all, it'll help me fall asleep. And I can't be hard up through all these fucking meetings...

2

After rubbing one out in the shower, a hard nap, and an afternoon filled with long-ass meetings, I'm ready for a drink. I take the elevator up to the presidential suite where, of course, she's staying for the weekend. She thought it would be better for us to meet up in private instead of hanging around in the lobby. So before our last meeting of the day, she slipped a spare key card into my pocket.

And even though I have my reservations about being alone with her, I decide she's probably right. Sneaking around is what we're best at, so I lean against the back wall of mirrors while I ride to the top of the building. The fourteenth floor is comprised of only the suite, making it the largest and most grand out of all the stays the Four Seasons has to offer.

It opens directly into the suite, showing off floor-to-ceiling windows everywhere you look. The dining area is right in front of me, with the kitchen to the left. I step further into the suite, and the doors close behind me.

"Coming!" I hear Ivy call out from what I assume is the

bedroom. A year ago, I would've made an inappropriate joke and followed her voice like my dick was a heat-seeking missile. Not now though.

"Take your time!" I call back.

"Is that what you're wearing?" she asks as she appears.

She's got on some wide-leg pants with heeled boots and a T-shirt that's tucked into the front of her jeans. She's got all of her hair down and hanging to the side as she puts in a pair of gold hoop earrings. I don't think I've ever seen her dressed so relaxed, and it's throwing me off. Even the expression on her face looks less intimidating.

Don't get me wrong, she's always been breathtakingly beautiful. But even in her most vulnerable moments, there was always a part of her that was closed off. I just chalked it up to her being my boss, but I'm starting to wonder if it was something else.

"Yeah?" I ask, looking down at my outfit. I'm still wearing my nice black pants and a button-up, but I only brought clothes to wear to business meetings. I didn't bring anything relaxed other than a T-shirt to sleep in.

She smiles and shrugs. "You still look good. Just makes me feel underdressed."

"What are you talking about? You look fantastic, Ivy."

She walks over to the kitchen and finishes a glass of wine that was sitting on the countertop. A whole glass of wine. She downs that like it's going to solve all the problems in her world.

"I thought we'd go downtown," she tells me as she wags her eyebrows. The glass clinks as she sets it back down on the marble.

"You want to go barhopping? I thought you wanted to go to dinner and catch up?" I ask, a little surprised. "You know it's just going to be a bunch of cowboys, bachelorette parties, and long lines, right?"

"Scared you can't keep up?" she asks, a mischievous look in her eye. "It's my birthday. I wanted to do something different."

Hell. I forgot it was her damn birthday weekend. Now I feel like shit.

"Then off to Broadway we go," I concede. It's the main drag of downtown Nashville. The best bars, the best barbecue, and the best live music. I've been before, and it can get fucking wild down there.

I hold out my arm for her to link with, and when she comes over, she wraps her arms around my torso and kisses me on the cheek. She smells like freshly picked fruit, and *fuck*, I really want to take a bite of it.

"I missed you." Her smile is wide as she looks at me, both of us just taking each other in for a moment.

You'd never guess she was a solid fifteen years older than me. She holds herself high, and she knows her fucking worth. Every time she walks into a room, she commands the attention of every man and woman. All eyes on her, all the time.

"Come on," she says, breaking the moment between us. She takes a little step away and links her arm through mine. "Let's go have a few drinks. Maybe I can convince you to line dance with me."

She winks, and I just laugh.

All the times we've gone out together, she's been desperate for me to dance. I don't dance. I am white. Very, very white. I can't carry a beat for shit.

"Not worried about people maybe seeing us together?" I ask her as we stand in the elevator.

I try not to look around and just focus on the numbers slowly lighting up as we descend because all of these mirrors are giving me the perfect view of her ass. All I can think about is pulling the emergency stop button and throwing her up against the wall. She could watch me as I kneeled at her feet and tugged those painted-on jeans over her thighs.

"I highly doubt these old men are going down to the honky-tonks." She laughs. "You're the youngest one of us here, you know."

"I noticed."

"It's impressive, Gregory." I feel her look up at me, but I keep my face forward and my eyes up on those damn numbers. I will not lose my fucking composure in this elevator. "You're really fucking good at what you do. Keep doing what you're doing, and maybe you'll fill my shoes one day."

"Not a fan of heels," I quip.

Her head dips back in laughter, and I chance a look down at the smooth column of her throat. Thank god the doors finally open, and fresh air swarms in.

"I'm serious," she continues as we walk out of the lobby. "You should be proud of what you've accomplished."

"I am."

She gives me a look.

"I am!" I insist, a smile playing across my lips. "I've worked my ass off to get here."

"Same." Her voice suddenly sounds a little tired, like she's lost some of her spark. "I'm tired of it."

Just when I'm about to ask her what she means, she speaks to the doorman to get a car brought around, and the words die on my tongue. It's none of my business. We aren't together. We're just friends going to get a drink together. I watch her as she laughs and jokes with the man while we wait for the car.

"Ready?" she asks, turning to face me when the car comes around. The wind makes her hair blow across her face, and I can't stop myself. It's a reflex to touch her. My hand reaches out and brushes it away, tucking it behind her ear.

I don't even notice that the driver has gotten out of the car to open the back door for us until he clears his throat. What the fuck is wrong with me? Why can't I just keep my goddamn dick in my pants for one night?

I can't even stop myself from ogling her ass as she climbs in, those jeans of hers cupping the curve of her hips perfectly. I know both of the men next to me are staring, too. Who wouldn't? But it sends a wave of jealousy through me, so I follow her in, effectively ending their free show.

The door shuts behind us, and I'm left alone with her and her sweet scent all over again. She pushes up closer to me, our thighs touching and the heat of her warming my own body. And then her hand—her fucking hand—goes to my leg and gives the muscles there a tight squeeze. She may as well have just grabbed my cock.

I groan, and a confident laugh falls from her lips.

I'm not going to survive this fucking night.

3

We get dropped off a few blocks away from Broadway, not wanting the car to have to fight its way through the people and the absurd amount of traffic they still allow down through the main drag. You'd think with the growing number of people visiting that they would shut it down at night.

The lights are bright, and the air is cool coming off the river. There are metal barricades that can barely contain the number of people on the sidewalks. They filter into the street, racing between the cars and laughing when they barely make it to the other side alive.

There's music pouring out of every single bar—all country, of course. This isn't really my scene. Our club back home caters to a completely different vibe. But Ivy's eyes light up as she takes in the raucous crowd. And I'm all about doing whatever she wants on her birthday.

"There's going to be a line no matter which one we try to fight our way into," I tell her, leaning close so that she can hear me over the people and the music. "Take your pick."

She decides on one that is lit up on the outside with pink neon with a live band on the inside. There's a bachelorette party in front of us, everyone color coordinated and wearing sashes. A group of guys in front of them tries to talk to them, but they're clearly drunk, and the girls just laugh and turn their backs on them.

Ivy crosses her arms and turns her back to the wind. It causes the sweet scent of her to surround me, and I finally stop resisting. I reach out and pull her close to me, spinning her around so that her back is to my chest. Wrapping my arms around her, I try to give her as much of my warmth as I can.

God, it feels good to have her in my arms again.

"You been doing okay?" I ask her. "You said you were tired earlier."

She sighs and lets her head drop back to my shoulder.

"There's a lot I've sacrificed to get to where I am." The group of guys gets let in as a large group comes out, and we move up, our bodies not separating. "I gave up relationships, getting married, having kids...having a life in general, honestly. I feel like I've given my entire life to this company, and in return, all I have is money to show for it."

"You regret it?"

She gives me a humorless laugh.

"Some days, I do. Some days, I look around my empty house when I come home, cook myself dinner, open a bottle of wine just to pour one glass, and think about how fucking quiet it is."

We move forward again as the girls in front of us file inside, the bride leading the way with a crown and her arms in the air in celebration.

"And then other times, I see a mother struggling with a toddler throwing a fit in one hand and a stroller in the other while she tries to open the door to Starbucks and think, *Thank god that isn't me*. Do you know how many times I've seen a mother struggling in public just to have not a single person help her, even though a dozen walk by?"

Too many to count, I'm sure.

"You could still have all of that," I tell her, kissing the side of her head. "You could scale back, try to meet the right person and settle down. You don't have to have kids to have a full life. But if you want a partner, make it happen."

She turns around in my arms to look up at me. I wonder for a second if she's going to say something about us. But just as she's about to say something, the bouncer calls us forward. We jump apart like we've been caught doing something illegal, but she just laughs it off and chats up the guy as she shows him her ID.

I don't know if it's just who she is or if it's from having to work with so many people over the years in the company, but she can make small talk with anyone. She knows how to make friends wherever she goes.

Once we're inside, the music is impossibly loud, and it's so full of people that I grab hold of her hand and make her hold on to my back pocket. I lead the way, fighting through the people to try and get to the bar. If I'm going to be forced to listen to country music all night, I'm going to need a few drinks in me.

"What'll it be?" The bartender yells in our direction once he finally makes his way over to us.

"Kentucky is known for its bourbon. Tennessee is known for, what? Whiskey? Should we get whiskey?" she asks, shouting over the music.

"Or moonshine," the bartender offers, smiling at her.

It plants a seed of jealousy in the pit of my stomach. She isn't mine. I do not own her. I do not have any type of claim to her whatsoever. But to see other men openly taking an interest makes me go a little crazy on the inside.

She used to love that about me—my possessive streak. Anytime we were in public, and I showed my ass because someone got a little too close or stared a little too long, she'd always drag me home to fuck for the entire night.

"Moonshine!" she cheers, her eyes lighting up. "Two shots each and a couple Coronas."

I lean in close, letting my lips brush against her ear. "Two shots each? Do you know what you're getting into with moonshine?"

Her head swivels toward me, and our mouths almost touch. Her pretty blue eyes dip to my lips, and she bites her own before looking back up at me. There's a crackle of electricity between us.

Our bodies are pushed close together with people on either side. Her chest is pressed up against mine, and her hand slides around my hips to settle inside my back pocket. That fucking smile she wears promises nothing but trouble.

"Never had it," she admits with a shrug. "But something tells me we might need it tonight."

The bartender comes back and sets everything down on the bar. She never takes her eyes off me as she holds a credit card out toward him between two fingers. I have no idea where she pulled that from, but the asshole inside of me is thrilled that she hasn't even looked in his direction.

There may be fifty other men in this bar that would crawl on their fucking knees to have a chance with her. But I already have.

We both grab a shot off the sticky bar and hold each other's eyes as we throw back the first shot. It burns the entire fucking way down, and I cringe when it hits my stomach and sets it on fire. When I breathe out, it lights up my entire fucking face.

And it must do the same to her because her face turns a deep red before she breaks eye contact and half laughs, half coughs, into her arm.

"Holy shit!" she says before picking up the second shot. "Let's get this shit over with."

She hands me mine, and we down the second shot. I don't know about her, but I have to fight the urge to let it all come back up. I'm not used to this shit. It's like drinking rubbing alcohol.

I cough once and reach out to grab the beer, hoping it'll dull the burn in my stomach. She's bent over in laughter, probably at how fucking red my entire face is as I desperately drink the beer to cool off.

"You should see your face!" she shouts over the noise.

"You don't look much better!"

"Dance with me!"

I groan and roll my eyes, but when the bartender shows back up, card in hand, I'm suddenly very eager to get her away from the bar.

"Alright, then," I concede, grabbing the Corona off the bar and holding out my hand. "Show me how it's done, country girl."

4

She takes my hand and pulls me to the middle of the dance floor. I feel incredibly out of place here. While I've been to a lot of different bars and clubs in my life, I've never been surrounded by so many people in cowboy boots.

She joins the line and motions for me to stand next to her. Our hands are clasped together between us, and we're holding our beers in the others. The live band announces a cover of Brooks and Dunn's "Boot Scootin' Boogie," and it appears we are all supposed to know the specific dance for this. Because everyone around us cheers and starts moving the second the song starts.

I've never even heard this song, let alone seen anyone dance to it. But Ivy seems to know exactly what she's doing. She looks over at me and gives me a nudge to follow her lead. She's in a fit of laughter while she watches me try to keep up. I'm stepping to the side, spinning and kicking, all while trying to fight the buzz from the moonshine and make sure I don't spill my beer.

Each time we spin, I let go of her hand, and once we right ourselves, she's right there, grabbing my hand again. Her head falls back in laughter over and over again, lighting up her gorgeous face. It's infectious, and I can't help but laugh at my stumbling feet as well. It's fun as hell, but shit if I don't suck at it.

"You're not very good!" she shouts over the music.

"No shit!" I shout back, trying to keep up as we do another spin.

But this time, I won't let her separate us. Instead, I give her a quick tug until she's stumbling and falling into me. I sit my beer on a high top next to us and do the same to hers before throwing both of her arms around my shoulders. She smiles up at me and bites her lower lip.

"You'd look hot in a cowgirl hat," I tell her, wagging my eyebrows as I tease her.

She just rolls her eyes and follows my lead as we do our best to stay out of everyone's way. Finally, the song changes, and the tempo slows. I pull her closer until almost her entire body is flush with mine as we spin in slow circles.

I never said I was a good dancer, but I've been to a few dances in school. I know how to do the basics. And she doesn't seem to be complaining. The neon lights shine on her silky black hair, and I can't stop myself from running my hands through the ends that hang around her waist.

"You know," she says, leaning closer so that I can hear her. "I think I'd like to see *you* in a cowboy hat. And maybe nothing else."

I swear to Christ every ounce of blood in my body races to my cock. There are too many memories between us for her to say that kind of shit and get away with it. I let my hands skim down from her waist to settle on the firm curve of her ass. When I give her a quick smack, she rears back and gives me a look that promises I'm going to pay for that.

And *fuck* if I don't want to.

Before she can say anything, I give her a little shove out from my body and spin her around before tugging her back in. Her hair flies around in a circle, and by the time she gets back to me, her lips are curved back up in a smile.

"Want some more moonshine?"

"You trying to get me drunk, Gregory?"

"Hey, it's your birthday," I say with a shrug. "I think we should celebrate."

She waits a beat and then nods, peeling away from me to sit at the high top where I left our beers. I lean over her and pick up the beers before going to the bar, and when I wink in her direction, her eyes are saying something that her mouth refuses to say out loud.

But I hear it loud and clear. We're both tempted to pick up where we left off. Not only tempted, but we really, really want to. Before I turn away, her eyes graze over my body and stick on the bulge in my pants. Even in the dim light of the bar, I can see her pupils widen. And then her tongue darts out and wets her bottom lip.

I'm not a cocky guy, but I love seeing the way she responds to me. I'd be lying if I said it didn't boost my ego a little.

"Be right back, mistress." My mouth is so close to her ear as I whisper they brush against the shell of it. Her entire body tenses and shivers. I haven't used that name since we were last together, and I know what effect it has on her.

I've only ever used it with her, and only ever while I was submitting to her.

And then I turn away and push my way to the front of the bar. Trying to get the attention of a bartender without a gorgeous woman next to me is a little more difficult, but one of them finally makes their way down. After ordering some more shots of moonshine, I try to make it back to her at the table without spilling anything.

The only thing is, when I manage to get out of the bar crowd, I see someone flirting with her. He's leaning over the table, getting up in her space while she smiles at him politely. Because of the music, he has to get close—too close—and I can feel my temper getting away from me.

My friends always give me shit for having the shortest temper of the bunch, but I can't help it sometimes. If someone pushes me too far, my blood pressure skyrockets, and I can't control myself. Especially when it involves this woman.

I'm frozen in place watching this interaction, trying to gauge her interest. I know that we aren't together anymore, so I know it's not my place to lose my ever-loving mind with jealousy. No matter how badly I *want* it to be my place.

Those pretty blue eyes slide from the man in front of her and find me staring at her like an idiot. And suddenly, I see the switch in her. She always has had a soft spot for my possessive nature. She loves teasing me, testing me. I suppose now is one of those times.

Because in a split second, she turns from just looking polite to looking like she wants this man to take her home and fuck her senseless. But that's not happening.

It'll be me that takes her home. It'll be me that fucks some goddamn sense into her.

She glances over his shoulder at me and smiles when she sees me down a shot. My girl knows what's about to happen, and she is fucking living for it.

My feet finally move from where they were rooted to the sticky floor, and I tap the guy on the back before handing her the shot I got for her. He leans away from her to look me over, and Ivy just downs the moonshine with a smile, anticipating my sudden mood change. Her legs cross, and I don't miss the way her thighs flex and squeeze together.

If I had to guess, she's wet just from the anticipation.

"Move along," I say calmly but loud enough he can hear it over the music.

He turns to look at me. "This your woman?"

I lean on the table and give him a once-over.

"Nope," I answer. She isn't, not anymore.

"Then move along." He makes a little *shoo* motion with his hands, and I swear Ivy nearly chokes on her shot.

"Look." I give him a hollow laugh. "This can either be fun for me and ugly for you, or you can just walk away and save the lady the show."

"Fuck off, bro." He gives me a little shove, and now I'm *actually* laughing. Because now I get to break his fucking hand.

I grab it before he can pull away, and I swing his arm around behind his back. Luckily, it's dark enough and loud enough that I don't draw any attention to us.

"What the fuck, man?" he squeals as he tries to fight against my grip.

"As much as I'd like to see it happen," Ivy says, catching my eye. "You don't own this bar, Gregory. This isn't California."

I look up at her, knowing she's right, but my temper is blinding me at this point. I squeeze his hand tighter, forcing his thumb to bend in an unnatural way. He gasps out in pain and raises up on his toes to try and get away from it.

I sigh in disappointment. If I break his hand, I'm looking at charges. I don't own this bar or have any sway with the cops around here. It's too big and too far away from home. And I'd like to spend the night with Ivy, not in jail.

"We're leaving anyway," I say. Ivy's lips pull into a smirk. "I don't wanna see you again tonight."

"Alright, man!"

I let him go and push him away. He stalks off, holding his wrist with tears in his eyes. Ivy snorts out a cute little laugh.

"Let's go, cowboy."

5

We barhop for the rest of the night, hitting up almost all of the places on Broadway until we kind of make friends with a group of people who know their way around the area. They're going off the strip to more local spots, and we're both just drunk enough to agree to go with them.

    Ivy hops onto my back as we walk outside, her laughter infectious as the other girls in the group join her by hopping onto their own men. She's three sheets to the wind, and if we're honest, I'm right behind her. I sway to the side, nearly dropping her but gaining my balance at the last second.

    The Uber is already there and waiting, and we all pile into this massive van that they've asked to take us to the next place. And, damn, they weren't lying when they said it was a hole-in-the-wall. You'd miss it if you didn't know what you were looking for, and if you did know, you'd probably still turn around and run the other way.

    There's a single red neon sign above some outdoor seating and a heavy black door. And that bouncer, Jesus fucking

Christ. The drunk in me wants to ask if I can pet his shiny bald head, but the reasonable side of me is screaming to keep my hands to myself.

The reasonable side wins, but not for Ivy. She skips over to him and works her magic, leaning up against him and rubbing his bald head like it's a magic fucking eight ball.

"Ivy," I growl under my breath, trying my hardest to not laugh in this man's face as I pull her away from him. He looks very unimpressed, but something tells me by the way he's fighting a smirk that he's not as pissed as he should be.

"What?" she squeals, giggling as I lift her off the ground. "He liked it. Didn't you, baby?"

He just rolls his eyes and lets us into the dimly lit dive bar. The smell of stale cigarettes and beer punches me right in the face, but I've been to hundreds of these places, and there's always something comforting about the way the small places treat you compared to the bigger clubs.

The group we're with heads straight to the bar, but Ivy pulls me to the dance floor and tugs me in close to her body. She smells like sweat and her shampoo, and I breathe her in as my hands roam over her soft curves.

"Tonight has been fun." It's much easier to hear her in here. There's a band playing here, too, but the crowd is much smaller, allowing us to not need to scream.

"Happy birthday," I tell her as I pull back slightly to look into her eyes.

She hums, her eyes struggling to stay fully open as we sway to the music. I lean forward and kiss her forehead. It's the most we've done except for the occasional butt slaps and our hands roaming. But the more drunk I get, the less I care that we've already tried to once. I want to try it again.

Or at least one more time.

"I've decided to retire," she blurts, an embarrassed smile

pulling at her lips. "God, that's sad. Retiring. When did I get so old?"

Her head drops to my shoulder, effectively hiding her face from mine. It takes my brain a second to catch up. Not because I think she should be embarrassed for retiring at her age but because she's *retiring*. She's leaving the company.

She isn't going to be my boss anymore.

"Your silence is reassuring," she grumbles.

"Hey." I chuckle and grab hold of her face to force her to look at me. "You should not be embarrassed that you are retiring. Do you know how many people would kill to be able to retire at your age? You are probably one of the youngest women in corporate America to retire."

"That's an overstatement, Gregory." She groans, but I can see my words have had some effect. She's less embarrassed now and more just...shy.

I spin her out and back in, over and over again until she's smiling again, and pull her back into my body tightly. She collapses into me with an *oomph*, but she's still smiling, and I'll take that as a win.

"I'm just tired of it," she explains. "I gave up a lot to get to where I am today. I ruined relationships. I spent way too much time away from my family. I gave up kids. All for this job that made me a lot of money, but not a lot of happiness."

"If you weren't happy, why'd you keep going?"

She shrugs.

"What else was I going to do? I was good at it—really good at it. And when I was younger, I was happy just making money. I thought I would never get sick of it. I had never met anyone that made me want to leave it, and I saw so many women hating their lives with a baby on their hip and a man on their arm."

She breathes out a laugh and looks away.

"That sounds so incredibly sexist against my own gender, I know. But I was adamant I would never want it. And I know plenty of women who are like me that *still* don't want it."

Her eyes swivel back in my direction.

"But I do."

"You do," I repeat back to her like an idiot. I'm dumbstruck.

"I do. Maybe not the babies," she says, clearing her throat and forcing out a laugh. "That ship has probably sailed. But I'd like to have a social life. To be able to date who I want to date without looking over my shoulder."

"Ivy." I drawl her name out, feeling my lips curl up into a grin. My hands tangle into the soft strands of her hair, and her head tips back just slightly. She wets her lips. "Are you saying you want to date me?"

Her eyes dip down to my mouth and then back up to my eyes.

"Are you saying you would?"

Instead of answering her with words, I answer her with a kiss. I'm gentle at first, testing the waters to see if this is what she actually wants. But the moment I pull back to check, she yanks me closer. Her mouth opens, and her tongue fights with mine for control. It's always like this, and I fucking love it—the fight for dominance.

Her hips roll and press up against mine, forcing a growl from deep in my throat as I devour her. There are people making all sorts of encouraging noises from behind me at the bar, and I can only assume it's the rowdy bunch that we came here with. Ivy breaks the kiss and flips them off over my shoulder. They all laugh and go back to whatever it was they were talking about.

"Want to go home?" Her fingers play with the ends of my hair at the back of my neck.

"Is that what you want?"

She laughs and rolls her eyes.

"I forgot," she says, curling her fingers through my belt loop. "You like it when *I'm* the one in control, don't you?"

She kisses me again, this time with more force. This time, she's not taking any fucking prisoners. Her tongue works mine over until her teeth come down and bite hard on my bottom lip. When she pulls away, I taste blood, and my cock is threatening to burst through my zipper.

"Well?" she asks. "You know I don't like to repeat myself."

"Yes," I say on an exhale. "Yes, I do."

"Good boy," she purrs against my lips. "Let's go home."

6

Before I can throw her over my shoulder and take her outside, one of the guys interrupts and begs me to join them for a game of pool. I'm about to tell him to fuck right off when Ivy interrupts and tells me to go play a game, and then we'll leave.

I look at her like she's crazy, but she just smiles. This is what she gets off on, being in control of the situation. She knows I'm hard as a rock in my pants, but making me wait is all part of the foreplay for her.

But I'm not as disciplined as she is. So when we're almost done with this godforsaken game of pool and she excuses herself to the ladies' room, I give it a second and then follow her, ordering a ride home on the way. I'm a stalker, hunting my prey through the bar like some sort of feral beast.

My blood is pounding a drumbeat in my ears, and my peripherals are blurry. I'm a man on a goddamn mission to taste that woman within the next three minutes, or I'll cease to exist.

I test the handle, but she's locked it, so I pound on the dirty wood door until she throws it open, looking for a fight. When she sees it's me, she just smirks.

"Can I help you?"

"You can."

I push her further in, locking the door behind us before shoving her against the wall with my hand on her throat. I pin her there, my thigh between hers and my mouth hovering over her lips. She's fisting my shirt at my sides, holding me tightly against her as I use my free hand to pull on a fistful of her dark hair.

Our bodies are so entangled that I can't tell where hers starts and mine ends.

"You can tease me all you want when we get back to the hotel," I murmur. "But right now, I need to taste you."

"Need?" she asks, still trying to come off as the one in charge—the one dominating this situation.

Instead of answering her, I kiss her. I attack her mouth, forcing it to open for me so that I can dip inside. Her whimpers and moans are like coming up for air. I've missed her body and her sounds. I've missed the way she melts into me every time we're together. I've missed *her*.

I keep kissing her as my hands move south to unbutton her jeans. The damn things are practically painted on, and I wind up ripping a belt loop in my haste to push them down her thighs. She breaks the kiss and laughs while my hands move to her now bare ass.

"Take it easy," she whispers, planting a soft kiss on my lips. "We have all night."

"We do," I agree. "But I told you. Just need a taste, baby."

My hand comes around and dips between her thighs, teasing her slit with my finger. She's bare, freshly waxed, and

I groan at the softness of her skin. And—fuck—she's wet. So, so wet.

Finding her clit, I gently circle it with the tip of my finger, relishing in the breathy moans coming from her mouth. Her arms wrap around my neck, and her fingers delve into my hair. She pulls hard, and that twinge of pain sends a jolt of pleasure down to my cock, making it pulse painfully against my zipper. It's a testament to my self-control that I don't fuck her right here, right now, against this wall.

Instead, I push deeper, letting one finger slide deep into her pussy. And then I add another, and another.

"Look at you," I murmur against her heated skin. I kiss down her jaw until I can nip at that sensitive spot next to her ear. "You're taking it so well. How's that feel, baby?"

"Yes" is all she manages to say.

A deep chuckle rumbles through my chest. I love it when she becomes this soft little puddle in my hands, and watching her as she slowly comes apart gives me the most intense pleasure I've ever experienced.

"Are you going to come for me, Ivy?"

She struggles to open her eyes with my fingers thrusting and curling in the perfect rhythm. But those baby blues finally lock onto me, and she nods.

I tsk, teasing her.

"Use your words, baby."

She groans in frustration, but it turns into a moan that's all pleasure.

"You're fucking annoying when you're up on your high horse. How's that for using my fucking words?"

I double down my efforts, and the noises between her thighs and her moans are the only thing filling this little bathroom we're in. Thank god it's a small bar with a one-room bathroom kind of setup because there is no way we wouldn't have gotten caught by now otherwise."

"You look so beautiful, Ivy." I kiss her cheek. "Your face is flushed, and your hair is a mess. I bet if I pulled up this shirt right now, those perfect nipples would be hard as rocks, begging to have my teeth around them, wouldn't they?"

"Yes." She hisses, and I feel her body begin to tighten up. That orgasm is building like a coiled spring, ready to explode.

"So perfect." I kiss her mouth and nibble on her bottom lip. "I can't wait to watch you come. Give me something to taste, baby. Come for me."

I curl my fingers just right, and as she's about to cry out, I kiss her. Her nails dig into the back of my neck while her pussy clamps down on my fingers. Our kiss softens, and once her body has relaxed, I slowly bring my fingers up to my mouth. They're shining wet from her release, and I let her watch as I lick each one of them clean.

"God, I missed this," I tell her as I suck the last of her juices from my third finger.

She licks her bottom lip and watches me the entire time. I know I'm going to pay for this when we get back, but I can't care. I like the punishment, and I can't wait to see what she has in store for me.

"You're in trouble."

I laugh.

"I figured. Sorry about the jeans," I say as I gently bring her thong and tight denim back up over her hips.

She leans forward and gives me the sweetest kiss, tasting herself on my lips.

"Ready to go back now?" I ask her. "No more games? No more torturing me?"

Her hand runs down my chest and over my abs before

settling on the steel fucking pipe between my legs. She gives it a squeeze, and stars flood my vision. I could come just from a single touch I'm so turned on right now.

"I guess." She shrugs and gives me a teasing smile.

"Finally," I groan.

I lean over and pick her up, tossing her easily over my shoulder. She squeals, and I hook my arm around the back of her knees before she can flail or kick. There's a bit of a line outside of the bathroom, and I should probably be ashamed. But when I have a woman this good-looking, nothing will stop me from getting what I want.

"Leaving?" one of the guys shouts from the bar. I can't be bothered to remember their names. I'm literally never going to see them again.

"Looks like it!" Ivy yells back, a fit of laughter pouring from her lips.

The bouncer snorts as we walk out. "Be safe, kids."

I salute him and stalk off toward our car.

7

The moment we're back in her hotel room, she is all business. That carefree woman that let me take a little bit of control throughout the night is gone. This is the woman I remember from last year.

"Kneel."

I don't waste a second. I drop to the hard tiled floor of her entryway and look up at her for approval. All I want is that little smile, the one that tells me I've done exactly as she's wanted. The floor biting into my knees is of little consequence.

"Good boy." She runs a hand through my hair and finally gives me that smile I've been looking for. "Stay here while I get changed. No relaxing, no sitting back on your heels. I want you to be uncomfortable. Think about all the bad things you did tonight, yes?"

"Yes, mistress."

Her pupils dilate. She loves it when I submit.

And when she walks into her room, I'm definitely *not*

doing as I was told. Because all I can think about is what she's changing into and what toys she might have brought with her. It might be stupid to hope she brought my favorite outfit—the shiny, tight, and oh-so-short black latex dress—but I can't stop myself from daydreaming about how fucking good she looks in that thing.

Especially when she's dragging her little leather crop across my body.

Christ, I'm going to get light-headed from all the blood draining to my cock. I've been hard for so long it's painful, and I know there's no way in hell she's going to let me come anytime soon.

"Give me a list," she calls out from her room.

I snap out of my daydream, wondering what kind of fucking list she's talking about.

"A list?"

She laughs, and I know I've fucked up.

"A list of all the things you were supposed to be thinking about, Gregory."

I swear under my breath.

"Well, the biggest mistake was probably taking control by shoving you against a wall by your throat?"

"Good. That's one," she answers.

"I also remember smacking your ass in public."

"Two." Her voice is closer. She's teasing me, not letting me see her until I've listed everything off.

"I almost broke someone's hand?" I'm not sure if that one counts, seeing as she normally likes it when my possessive side comes out.

"Normally, I like that side of you," she murmurs. She's close now, and it's taking every ounce of self-control to not turn around. I'm dying to know what she's wearing. "But seeing as we aren't in your domain, I think it was a little too bold of a move."

"That's three, then," I tell her. "What do I win?"

Another dark laugh comes from her.

"You're missing one."

Am I? Shit. I can't think of anything else, especially once I hear the clicking of her heels as she gets closer. She's so distracting. I can't fucking focus.

She walks up right behind me, and I feel the heat from her body as she leans over to speak in my ear.

"You questioned whether or not I could hold my liquor when it came to the moonshine. Never question me. Especially in public."

S*hit.* Forgot about that.

"Yes, mistress."

Her hands run over my shoulder blades, over my shoulders, and around to my chest. Slowly, she begins to unbutton my shirt until her palms can run across my collarbone and down to my abs.

"I have a surprise for you," she whispers.

Dear God, if you let this surprise be that little black dress I love so much, I will do your bidding for the rest of my fucking life.

"I was hoping we would reconnect on this trip," she continues. "And I thought if we did, you might appreciate me bringing your favorite outfit."

"Oh, fuck yes," I say on an exhale.

"Do you think you deserve to see me in it?"

"Probably not, but I'm not above begging."

8

A deep laugh rumbles through her, dripping in sex.

"I like it when you beg."

My cock throbs in my pants, and the cold tile bites into my knees. I know better than to move and readjust myself, but if she doesn't give me *something*... Her hands leave my body, and I exhale, trying to settle my nerves. I haven't slipped into any type of subspace since the last time we were together, and it takes a moment to reroute my brain from being in charge to being able to let go.

It's a relief when it happens—the letting go. It's like my brain goes quiet, and the aches and pains in my muscles are dulled. But at the same time, my senses are heightened. I can hear her soft breathing behind me, the pleasurable pain in the way my dick presses against my zipper, and I can feel her waiting not so patiently for me to do as I've been asked to do.

"Please," I start. "I'm begging you, mistress. I need to see you in that dress. When I close my eyes, I can still see how it hugs every curve on that gorgeous body and the way it pushes your tits together in the most bitable way."

"Almost." I can hear the smile in her voice.

"I will do anything to see you in that dress, Ivy. I will crawl to you. I will kiss your feet. I will give you so many orgasms you can't even stand after. I will do *anything* for you to let me see you."

"Oh, I like the sound of that."

Her heels click as she walks in slow strides to stand in front of me. I don't turn my head, even though I want to. But I know this is all part of it, waiting until *she's* ready. But she's moving so fucking slowly. If this was anyone else, I would reach out and pull her to me.

"As good as you remember?"

She's finally standing directly in front of me in that tight-as-fucking-sin black latex dress. The heeled boots are black and go all the way up to the middle of her thigh. And the dress hugs her hip dips perfectly, showing off the roll of her stomach and the scoop of her waist. Her tits are pushed together and held high by the tight fabric, and I can't wait for her to smother me.

"Fuck," I breathe out. "You look good enough to eat."

"That can be arranged." She smirks and turns her back on me, walking into the living room. God, her ass looks phenomenal. Round and so fucking peachy that I feel my mouth water as it sways with her hips.

She sits down on the sofa and runs her hands down her thighs, tempting me when she hasn't released me yet. I can feel myself leaning forward, like she's magnetic. Slowly, her hands pull her knees apart, opening her thighs to expose her sweet cunt. She's not wearing panties, showing me how wet she is already.

A whimpering noise escapes my lips. I can't fucking help it. I'm starving for her.

"Crawl to me, baby."

She doesn't have to tell me twice. I move immediately, falling forward and letting my hands catch me. I crawl on my hands and knees across the room, my eyes never leaving that sweet, glistening spot between her legs.

"Stop," she says as I get close enough to smell her arousal. My head is between her thighs, and I'm so fucking close. A weaker man wouldn't listen. A weaker man would dive in and enjoy his fucking meal.

But I'm not weak.

At least, that's what I tell myself to stay still.

Strong. Big, strong man. I can do this.

She chuckles.

"Your thoughts are written all over your sweet face, you know that?"

"It doesn't surprise me." I glance up at her, just struck by how fucking gorgeous this woman is. Her eyes are practically glowing as she looks down at me with her dark hair falling over her shoulders.

"Tell me what you want," she says, her voice husky from arousal. Her tongue swipes at her bottom lip before her teeth bite down on it.

"I want to dive into that sweet cunt, mistress. I want to spread those lips with my tongue and suck hard on your clit, just how you like it. I want to tease you with my fingers until you're screaming my name and pulling my hair—until your body gives in and comes all over my face. I want you to squeeze my head with your thighs until I can't breathe. Fuck my face. Use me. Please. Fuck. Please, use me."

Her hands dig into my hair, and she tugs me forward, losing her control. She does exactly as I wanted, squeezing her thighs around my ears and shoving my face so deep in her pussy I struggle to breathe.

She's drenched, her juices coating my entire face as she rides me. The sweet noises she makes as I pleasure her with my tongue drive my own desire and pleasure higher. Even though she isn't touching my dick, I feel like I could explode on the spot. I try to move my hips to get some friction on my pants, and she spots it, laughing as she leans forward to swat my ass.

"Like a bitch in heat."

I don't do anything but growl and dig deeper in response. She's right. I'm in heat. And she's the only one that can cool me the fuck off.

Moving so that I can balance on one hand, I adjust my other to tease her with the tips of my fingers. She goes crazy for this, when I only tease her entrance, not giving her what she wants. I circle around her pussy as I suck on her clit, pushing her closer and closer to the edge.

I'm on a mission to get her to come in record time, so when I know she's ready, I slip a single digit deep into her pussy and curl it against her G-spot. I pulse against it, making her cry out. Her thighs squeeze tighter, and her stomach moves and flexes with how hard she's breathing.

"Good boy," she breathes. "Yes, baby. That's right. Right there. Make your mistress come all over that tongue. Just like that."

I groan. I fucking love it when she talks like this, working her way to her orgasm while also praising the shit out of me. I add another finger, scissoring and pressing deep inside of her.

Finally, she screams, her release flooding my mouth. I lap at her, making sure not to quit too soon but not pushing her too far. She gets sensitive fast, and I don't want to move too fast tonight. I want to savor it.

"Fuck yes," she coos, running her hands through my hair as she praises me. "You are so good at that, aren't you? Such a good boy for me."

And then her fingers tighten in my hair, yanking me back away from her while her thighs fall away from my head. I pant, trying to catch my breath as she forces my head back to look at her.

"You're so handsome like this, you know that?" she asks, but I'm still trying to catch my breath. "I love it when you're on your knees, your face covered in my cum, and desperate for your own release."

I can't do anything but sit here on all fours and pant. I'm so turned on that I can't form thoughts. My cock is throbbing, and my balls ache with the need to spill inside of her.

"I think I should get a toy to play with. What do you think, sweet boy?"

I swallow.

"Yes, please."

She grins.

"Good."

9

I follow her to the bedroom on my hands and knees, crawling behind her like the good little subservient I am. She hasn't told me I could get up yet, so I follow her quietly like this.

I think about what my friends would think if they knew I was like this with her. I've never, ever been like this with anyone except her. Normally, I'm the dominant one, taking control of the situation and making their bodies bend to my will. Not the other way around.

But from the first moment Ivy and I messed around with each other, this dynamic seemed to work for us. It was like I had been waiting for someone like this my entire life. Someone needed to wake up this side of me.

And I don't think anyone would judge me for it. I mean, shit, just look at her. Who wouldn't want to be crawling on their knees through a presidential suite, waiting to have the best sex of their life? But I do think the guys would be surprised, seeing as I'm the total opposite when it comes to daily life.

"Pay attention!" A hard smack on my ass brings me back to the moment, the sting resonating through my stomach and spine as my balls tighten.

"I'm sorry, mistress." I bow my head, letting it fall toward the floor until her booted feet appear in front of me. She lifts one slightly off the ground.

"Kiss it for forgiveness."

Her voice is quiet, just a murmur, but it holds so much power over me. I don't even hesitate. My head dips lower, and my lips graze the soft material of her boot. And after I've kissed my way up from the toe to her ankle, I risk looking up at her with a smirk. Because I may submit to her, but that doesn't mean I'm not a brat.

"If you had a foot fetish, Ivy, you could've just asked. I'm happy to have a play with these pretty feet."

She snorts, and a hand flies to her mouth as she tries hard not to dissolve in a fit of laughter. And I just stare up at her, admiring just how fucking gorgeous she is from any angle.

"You're a little shit," she says when she can finally contain her laughter again.

I shrug and then continue to kiss up her calf. Her hands run gently through my hair, and her entire body softens when I reach her thighs.

"Can I ask what toys you brought?"

I bite down on the zipper of her left boot and tug it down, finishing it off with my hand before doing the same with the other. Slowly, I pull each of her feet out of the heels, giving both of them a little massage before placing them on the ground.

"Your favorite crop and my favorite wand. I wanted to bring the sex swing, but that would have been a little too awkward to pack in a carry-on."

"You fit everything in a carry-on?" I tease her, and she

just rolls her eyes. Moving up onto my knees, I let my hands roam up her thighs and under the tight dress she's wearing. Her skin is so soft, so fucking smooth. I place a kiss on her inner thigh, and she sighs.

"It's just a weekend. I didn't think I needed much."

"And you didn't know if you'd see me."

"I hoped I would," she tells me, her fingertips running down my cheek. "I've wanted to reach out for ages. The day we decided to break it off was not a good one for me."

She takes a deep breath, and when I meet her eyes, they're filled with unshed tears. Without worrying about whether or not she wants me to stand, I do. I'm not going to sit here on my knees while she's expressing all of these emotions I've never seen from her before. When we were messing around, it always just seemed like something we were doing for fun. Nothing more.

But the way she's looking at me right now says something totally different.

"Hey." My voice is soft, like I don't want to startle her or scare her away from facing the feelings she's clearly trying to sort through. "It's okay."

"I missed you." She blinks, and a few tears escape to fall down over the soft curve of her cheeks.

"I missed you, too, you know. And not just the sex. I missed *you*."

"I figured this was just something fun for you. Like a friends-with-benefits sort of thing."

"Friends with benefits? With my boss? I think it would have to be considered something a little more than that when you take into account how much shit we could've gotten into for it." I smile at her and wipe the tears off her cheeks. "It was a lot of risk to take—still is."

"Not if I'm not your boss anymore."

"That's a huge step to take just because you like someone, Ivy."

"I'm not quitting for you." She groans and gives me a playful shove. "You're just a bonus. It's like the opposite of a signing bonus. My quitting means I get to keep you around."

"Like a pet?" I ask her, smirking when she just rolls her eyes again.

"You are *such* a little shit, do you know that?"

I laugh and pull her body into mine. Now that the heels are off, she fits against me like a missing puzzle piece.

"Shut up and kiss me, boss lady."

Lifting herself up on her tiptoes, she kisses me. Her lips are soft and gentle before it becomes more urgent. She opens her mouth to me, and our tongues explore before my teeth bite down on her lip.

My arms wrap around her waist, lifting her off the ground enough to step backward until we're at the bed. We both lie down, me on top of her, and our hips automatically begin to grind. Her hands are everywhere, frantically pulling at my hair and then tugging at the back of my shirt. I finally free myself of it after a lot of falling all over her.

The feel of her hands on my bare skin is euphoric, and when her nails scratch down the muscles of my back, I roughly arch into her. I can feel the heat between her thighs through the material of my pants, and I'm not sure how much longer I can wait. At least for this first round.

"Fuck it," she moans in between kisses. "I know you want to. I know you're thinking about it. Just fuck me, baby. I know you're good for another round."

I pull back slightly, and she winks at me before her hands are working hard at my belt and pants. She uses her feet to push them off my hips, and when my cock finally bobs free, it rests against her slick center.

She watches as I stroke myself a few times before lining the head up with her clit and teasing her. I press against it, circle it, and dip just barely inside of her until she's a moaning, breathy mess. Her heels dig into my ass as she tries to urge me on.

"First," I say as I tug her dress down under her breasts with my other hand. "First, I want to free these gorgeous tits. I want to see them bounce as I fuck you hard into this mattress."

Her nipples are hard, and when I lean forward and suck one into my mouth, her back arches. I take as much of it as I can into my mouth, making a mess as I bite and lick her entire breast. When I move to the other, her nails dig painfully into my biceps.

"Fuck me," she growls. "I can't take it any longer."

A laugh rumbles out of me and vibrates against her skin.

"All you had to do was ask."

10

I line up with her and slowly sink inside. Fuck, I have missed this.

"God, Ivy." I moan into the crook of her neck, my breath hot against her throat. "This pretty little pussy is taking me so well. Tight. Wet. Fuck."

I grab her hands and push them above her head, holding her wrists together with one hand while I use my other to play with her nipples. Her legs are wrapped around me and hold me close as I begin to thrust inside of her. I start slow, teasing and torturing her as her hips try to grind against me.

"I forgot just how big you are," she says with a little laugh. A bead of sweat rolls down her temple.

I halt my hips. "Need me to stop?"

"No." She frees her wrists and flips us over so that she's on top. "I just want a turn to hold the reins."

She rests her hands on my chest and lowers herself on top of me. Being able to watch her body take me like this is such a turn-on. She's soaked, and her walls clamp down around me as I sit fully inside of her.

When she begins to move, I lick my thumb and use it to play with her clit. She loves light touches and slow circles. It drives her body crazy. I watch all of her—her hips, her breasts, and her lips, which are slightly parted. Her blue eyes are closed as she focuses on her pleasure.

That's something I've come to love about this woman. She doesn't apologize for taking what she wants and doing what she needs to reach her orgasm. She isn't loud, and she doesn't like a whole lot of eye contact. When she's really feeling it, I know, because her eyes are closed and her breaths become deeper and slower, like she's prepping her body for what's about to happen.

And I get to watch it all. I get to watch her, pushing her in all the right directions while the pleasure sweeps through her. She leans back, resting her hands on my thighs.

"God, that's so sexy, Ivy," I tell her. "I love watching you take me. So good."

The faster she moves, the more those full tits bounce and the sloppier the sounds in the room get. I grab ahold of her hips and thrust to match her stride. I fuck her from underneath, letting her relax just a bit more into it.

"I'm coming," she whispers. Her head falls back, exposing the long column of her throat.

"That's it, Ivy. That's it."

"Right there!" she cries out. "Do. Not. Fucking. Stop."

I smirk, loving that even in the throes of an impending orgasm, she's bossy as shit.

A few seconds later, she's coming, and her body seizes up on top of me. One of her hands goes to her hair, tugging on it while her hips roll and grind. I flex every muscle in my body to keep from coming. Before I finish, I want another one from her. It's been so long since I've got to have her I don't want to waste it.

She flops to the side, breathless and laughing as I pull her back to me. Ivy fits so perfectly, her soft curves conforming against my hard muscles. Our skin is sticky with sweat as we lie here, just kissing softly and smiling at each other in between.

"Are you going to come anytime tonight?" she asks, her eyes taunting me.

I narrow mine on her.

"I planned to let you have one more. I wanted you to be well and truly fucked before I gave in."

"That sounds lovely." She hums. "How do you want me?"

She throws a leg over my hips, and I land a hard smack on her ass before forcing her to roll onto her stomach. I get behind her before she can protest and lift her hips. When she tries to lift herself up onto her hands, I push her head back down into the mattress.

"I told you I was going to fuck you deep into this bed, Ivy." I slap her ass again. "I intend to keep that promise."

I push inside of her, watching as her cunt stretches wide to accommodate me. My balls are already tightening, and I know I'm not going to hold out for long. Reaching around to her clit, I tease her sensitive nub until I feel her walls tightening from the overstimulation.

Her hands hold on to the sheets until her knuckles turn white, and I fuck her hard and deep, using her dress to hold on to as leverage, until she struggles to keep her body upright to match my thrusts. Our skin slaps together, and her little whimpers and whines fill the room. She's breathing heavily, and her ass is pushing back on me to try and take everything I'm giving her.

"I can't."

"You can," I tell her. "Take a deep breath for me, love. Let it go."

For once in her life, she does as she's told, relaxing her body to let the orgasm take over. The second she does, I'm right behind her. The heat spreads from my balls up my spine as I spill inside of her.

Using my thumbs to spread her ass apart, I watch as I come down from the high, as her pussy pulses around my dick. My cum begins to leak out, and it's the sexiest fucking thing I've ever seen. Seeing both of our releases mixing together as her tight entrance throbs around me.

I smack her again.

"Do you know how fucking sexy you look? This tight black dress still wrapped around your waist, my cum leaking out of this pussy. Fucking sexy."

"I don't easily blush," she says, slipping out of my grip as she lets her body relax into the bed. "But sometimes the shit that comes out of your mouth." She laughs.

"You love it."

After another playful love tap on her ass cheek, I roll off the bed and go hunting for something to clean her up with. I let the water get warm and then wet a washcloth. She's lying on her back when I walk back into the room, and she watches as I dip between her thighs to wipe away the mess I made.

"You're the first to ever do this. Did you know that?"

"To clean you up post-sex?" I ask, cleaning myself up once I'm done with her.

"Yeah." She sighs. "I think it's a younger man thing. Older men expect you to thank them for the mediocre ride and go get them a beer."

I snort. "That cannot be true. You've just had some duds."

"Maybe." She shrugs.

I toss the cloth to the side and crawl back onto the bed. We get comfortable, pulling some covers over us as we lie in the dim light that's flooding in from the main rooms. The wind whips around the windows outside, but it's pretty quiet for a hotel. I guess it is pretty late, and most people who stay here are on business trips, asleep before midnight.

She rolls onto her side and lays her head on my chest. I feel her body melt into mine as she takes a deep breath and runs her fingers through my chest hair. It's starting to get weird—the silence. I feel like it's gone on too long, but once you get to this point...who is supposed to break it? How do I break it?

"Your thoughts are so loud they can hear them in reception."

I laugh because it's probably true. I was stuck inside my head on a loop.

"I'm starving."

"It's like, two in the morning," she says. "Think they'll still have room service?"

"I was thinking more along the lines of Chinese..."

"Brilliant. You're a brilliant man!" She kisses my cheek and rolls off the bed, tugging her dress off as she goes. "No wonder I hired you," she throws over her shoulder before walking out into the living room.

"Funny!" I call out.

"I know!" she yells back. "Now, come tell me what you want!"

11

We couldn't find a single Chinese place open, but we did find an amazing late-night barbecue place that was close by. They didn't deliver, so Ivy sent her car to go get it for us. I tried to tell her that wasn't *really* what he was on call for, but she shooed me away, saying he loved her and would happily go get her drunk ass some food.

"So," she says between bites. "Tell me what I've missed in your life. How are your friends? Anything new and exciting?"

"Well, Aurora had a baby. That's Owen's and Hudson's partner. Turns out she got pregnant during that Tokyo trip, actually." I laugh, thinking about how they all really wanted a kid, and *boom*, they got one.

"Aww." She smiles. "Boy or girl?"

"Girl. Lucia, but she goes by Lucy most days. Cutest little thing. Almost gives me baby fever...almost."

"Mm," she hums. "They'll do that when you're able to hold them while they coo and giggle but give them back once they start acting up."

"Jack and Quin have been trying for the past year, but..." I trail off. It's not something they really talk about with us. We all know they're trying, and we know that seeing the happy family with their brand-new baby is rough. "They might try IVF next year. I think Quinlan is just trying to decide if she wants to put her body through that."

Ivy nods, her face serious. "I've heard the side effects can be brutal. Pregnancy is hard enough on a woman's body. Have they thought about adopting?"

I shrug. "They don't talk about it often. Not that I blame them. It's not our business, but I do think about them a lot. If I was a praying man, I would pray for them."

"Lucky for you, I am. I'll add them in."

"What?" I feel like she just slapped me. She has never, ever let on that she is a religious woman. The subject has never come up, and in my experience, Christians try to throw it into every conversation they can.

"Don't be so dramatic." She laughs. "I'm not going to try to convert you. Your faith, or lack thereof, is not something to fix."

"No, it just—it caught me off guard. I don't think you've ever brought it up before. I figured it would have in the time we spent together."

She shrugs and takes another bite of barbecue.

"Like I said, I'm not here to convert you. I believe in God, you don't. Not a big deal, Gregory." She gives me a teasing look.

"You never said anything about Pyro and his...situation." I can't get past it. I grew up in a religious family, and I know just how intolerant they can be. Especially when it comes to people like Pyro, Owen, and Aurora. But she never said a thing. She always accepted them like they were people.

It's such a stark difference to what I'm used to it's hard to connect the dots in my mind.

"Why wouldn't I?" she asks. "They're people. I'm not a bigot or a homophobe. People can love whoever the hell they want to love, and they're still loved by my God. If God made everyone in his image, that means he made Hudson and Owen and Aurora. He made you and me. So there's no reason to treat anyone any differently. That's just ignorance."

"I'm sorry." I can tell my line of questioning and my obvious doubt in her character has fucked with her a bit. Her mood is down, and she's not really looking at me. "Hey, Ivy."

She looks up at me.

"I'm sorry. I didn't mean to insinuate you were a bad person. It was a gut reaction. I was just taken by surprise."

"I feel like you've known me for long enough that you know my character," she says, her face serious. "Just because I happen to believe in something doesn't change anything about me."

"You're right." I reach across the little gap in between us where all the food sits and squeeze her hand. "I was stupid. I'm sorry. I'm just not used to seeing a Christian be so open-minded."

"We're out there," she says, her smile coming back. "You just have to look a little harder. The assholes tend to outshine us."

I sit up on my knees and lean over to kiss her. She tastes tangy and sweet.

"What about Wes? Where is he these days?"

I plop back down on my side. "God, I don't even remember. They're off in South America somewhere, I think. I think they've been home in California maybe twice in the past year. They are constantly on the move."

"They're happy though," she says with a wistful smile.

I return it. "They are. Everyone is."

"And you?" Her eyes flit to me and back to her food. "Are you happy?"

I shrug. "I've been as happy as I can be. If I'm honest, ever since things with us ended, I've been sort of...confused? Not sure if that's the right word. I don't know. I'm just not really sure what I'm doing."

"In life or in work?"

"Life. Work, I love. You know I love this job. But I watch all of my friends and their partners and the families that they're building. And I guess I'm just starting to feel a bit on the outs."

"It's hard being the last one in the group to not be *attached*." She uses air quotes on the last word. "It happened with me a lot. Lost a lot of friends because of it. Not in any malicious sort of way. But we just drifted apart. Interests change, and it's hard to not feel like the third wheel everywhere you go."

God, I can hear the sadness in her voice. My friends do a really good job of not making me feel left out. I'm always hanging out with them, going to their houses or vice versa. We do so much shit together, and they make sure not to treat me any differently. But I can see what she means about changing interests. I find myself not knowing how to talk about diapers or tricks to get pregnant.

At the end of the day though, they're still my family. I can't imagine losing them, and to know Ivy has gone through that multiple times is fucking sad. She has given up so much for this career. No wonder she's ready to retire early. Shit, she has the money for it.

"I'm sorry, Ivy. That shit is hard."

She shrugs and grins at me. "It is. But I'm hoping it's going to get a little easier. Retiring, maybe keeping in touch with you...if you'd like that."

I try to get her to look at me, but she is really finding that food interesting. I pick up a still-sealed plastic fork and knife packet and chuck it at her. And I have a phenomenal aim. That thing hits her right in the center of her forehead. She gasps and looks up at me, a shocked smile on her open mouth.

"That was rude."

"You wouldn't look at me. And I wanted you to be looking at me when I answered your question."

"What question?" She raises an eyebrow.

"Don't play coy now, boss lady. About you and I keeping in touch. Maybe...dating even?"

"Oh, right. That one."

"I'd like that."

Her eyelashes are long when she looks over at me from under them. There's a soft pink blush lighting up her cheeks, and I know it's taking everything in her to not look away right now. My dominant woman has a shy side, and I love how she is the best of both worlds, switching it up at a moment's notice.

"Yeah?"

"I would," I tell her. "I've got another business trip I'm leaving for after this one. But I would love to see you when I get home."

I push the food out of the way and crawl over to her, taking her mouth with mine and tangling my fingers in her hair. It's so long and soft, it's perfect to wrap around my fist and tug. I break the kiss.

"And we still have the rest of tonight."

She smirks.

"And toys we haven't used. It would be a shame to let those go to waste. Don't you think?"

"I thought you'd never ask."

12

Without all of her usual toys at our disposal, she's made great use of the pillowcases to tie my hands to the headboard and cover my eyes like a blindfold. My legs are still free, but I'm being a good boy and keeping them spread for her like she asked. I'm butt-ass naked, my cock is standing at full mast, and my mind is running with the possibilities of what her next move is going to be.

I hear her mess around in what I assume is her bag, and then she moves closer to the bed. I jump when the cool leather of my favorite little crop touches my bicep. She moves it slowly down my arm, over onto my chest, and down my stomach. My cock weeps in anticipation.

"Someone is excited," she murmurs as she teases the underside of my dick. Three little love taps have my ass flexing and my hips pushing to the ceiling.

That earns me a very hard slap to my inner thigh.

"Ah, ah," she scolds. "I said no moving."

I bite down on the inside of my lip and wait for her to

continue. The inside of my thigh is stinging like a bitch, but I don't mind the pain. I realized quickly with her that pain—to a certain extent—heightens my pleasure. I'm not into anything too severe, but I can handle what she wants to give me, and I can't lie, the best orgasms I've ever had have been with her.

She knows just how to push me right to my limits. We have a safe word; we established one the moment we stepped outside of my comfort zone. But I've never had to use it because she just *knows*. It's like she's so in tune with my body that she knows when I'm about to have enough, when I'm right at the edge of not being able to take any more.

If I do ever have to use it though, I know she'll stop immediately. I trust this woman wholeheartedly.

"Ticklish?" she asks as she runs it across the bottom of my feet.

I am. I am ticklish. But she told me not to move. So I'm biting my lip so hard I taste blood, refusing to show I'm affected.

She laughs softly.

"Good boy."

That's right. I am a good fucking boy.

The mattress dips between my legs as she crawls onto the bed and situates herself between my legs.

"What a sight, Gregory." The crop runs up my other leg and settles at my hip. "I like having you all naked and vulnerable, hands tied up and blindfold on."

The crop smacks against my hip, and I twitch, but it's small. She lets it go. Fuck, I forgot how much that shit stings. May as well hit me with a belt or a wooden spoon.

"Look how excited you are." I feel the soft leather of the crop move close to my cock, and the precum drips onto my abs, making a sticky mess.

Tap. Tap. Tap.

Three quick, light taps on my cock from the sensitive head to the base. My balls tighten, and my abs jump. That feels fucking phenomenal. With my eyes covered, every other sense is heightened. And everything she is doing makes me want to beg for release.

"Do you like that, baby?" she asks. "Do you like it when I give your cock a little pain?"

"Yes," I answer immediately, my voice sounding hoarse from the excitement. "I do."

A raspy chuckle escapes her lips, and it frightens and excites me at the same time.

"Should we see how much you can take, then?"

Fuck. This is where knowing I can use the safe word at any time brings me the confidence to let her move forward. Because even though her question may not have seemed like an actual question for consent, it was. She needs it to move forward. Ivy would never do anything against my will.

"Yes, mistress."

"Good boy, Gregory."

The crop moves to the side of my cock, and she begins with light touches, alternating from side to side. I know they're just going to get harder, so I try to control my breathing. Holding my breath only makes it worse and gets me in trouble.

As the delicate taps become harder, the stinging gets worse. The blows are landing all around my cock and balls. My thighs, my hips, and all around my cock—all without actually touching it.

My breathing is heavier as I try my hardest not to move, but my brain is torn. My body is feeling pain and pleasure, and my ass is desperate to flex while my hips are begging to roll up against something. My cock needs relief, and she refuses to give it.

"Keep breathing for me, baby," she says.

And then the crop lands on my dick.

"Fuck!" I shout, not able to contain it. Because that fucking *hurt*. But within seconds, the stinging fades, and all that's left is a burning hot sensation that makes me want to come on the spot.

"Okay?" she asks, giving my skin a second to breathe and my muscles a chance to relax. "Do we need to say the safe word?"

I take another deep breath.

"No," I answer. "No, I'm good. Do it again. Please."

"A slut for pain, aren't you?" The crop whacks against my dick again. "*My* little slut for pain," she almost growls.

I whimper, fighting through the pain to feel that glorious fucking warmth again. Blood pours to my cock and balls, making me so hard it hurts. My dick twitches, and there's a puddle on my stomach where it lies.

"Can you handle one more, you think?" Another consent question, but her tone is all domme, mocking and fascinated at the same time. But underneath it, she's waiting for the safe word or for consent.

"Yes." I grit the word out, knowing that she is probably the closest she's ever pushed me to using it. But I don't want to. I want to see how much I can take.

I hear the crop move through the air before I feel it. The pain is intense. My abs clench, and I'm pretty sure my balls disappear inside of me, hiding from the assault she's wreaking on my body.

But then she's there, her cool hand running over my heated skin, applying pressure and kissing away the pain. The crop clatters to the floor, and her mouth runs over the areas on my thighs while her hand soothes my abused cock. The long strands of her hair run against my heated flesh and tickle the sensitive spots.

"You did so well." Her breath floats across the head of my cock, and then her lips wrap around it, sucking me inside.

I hiss, and my hips press up, thrusting deeper. She lets me and runs her hands from my thighs up to my stomach, all while letting me fuck her face. Her teeth skim across the underside of my cock where all of the blows landed, and the little reminder of that pain pushes me even higher.

She moans around my cock when it slips into the back of her throat, and she runs her nails harshly down my front.

"Jesus Christ, Ivy." I grunt.

She pops off with an audible sucking sound.

"You taste so good." She's out of breath, and I'm desperate to lay my eyes on her. I want to see those pretty blue eyes all wild with lust. "You had my mouth watering this whole time, watching you drip for me."

Her nails dig into my hips as she pulls herself up my body. Gently, she unties the makeshift blindfold and tugs it away from my face. When I'm finally able to see her, my arousal only skyrockets.

Ivy's cheeks are flushed, and her hair is a mess. Her pupils are dilated as she looks down at me and bites that sexy lower lip.

"You've got me all riled up, Gregory."

She moves her body higher, getting her tits close enough to my mouth that I can suck and bite on each one before she shuffles higher. Her knees settle on either side of my face.

"I think you should help me with that."

13

My girl knows how to ride my fucking face.

There's none of this hovering bullshit because she's worried she might suffocate me. Ivy sits on my face and grinds against my nose. Her hands are gripping the headboard, and her head is thrown back in ecstasy. The view I have is magnificent.

I love everything about her body. And from this angle, I get to see the round curve of her belly that leads up to those amazing breasts. Her breathing is labored, and her hips are grinding, making her breasts bounce softly in time with her body. The long column of her throat is on display, and when her face moves to look down at me, I get to watch every little expression on her face as she uses me for her pleasure.

And her taste—fuck, her taste—is so goddamn sweet. I've missed pleasuring her with my tongue. She's so responsive. When I dip my tongue deep inside of her, her mouth opens to let out the softest moan. And when the tip teases circles around her clit, she bites her bottom lip.

Best of all, when I suck that little nub into my mouth, she praises me just how I like.

"That's it," she pants as I suck and suck. "Right there, baby. You know exactly how I like it, don't you?"

One of her hands comes down to play softly with my hair, twirling it between her fingers and tugging it gently at the roots. She does this sometimes after she's been rough. Her touches become delicate and loving, like she's reassuring me that it's not always going to be whips and chains. That she can be loving and soft as well.

I've never really dominated her before. That moment tonight in the bathroom was the first time I had really ever taken control. But sometimes I wonder if she would like to be a switch with the way her demeanor changes mid-activity sometimes.

But then I remember the way she looks at me when I *do* try to take some control, and I remember that that probably isn't what she wants...

"Fuck, baby."

She throws her head back again, and I can tell she's getting close. Her breaths pick up, and she starts to go silent. The grip her fingers have on my hair tightens, and I just keep doing what I'm doing. I know better than to switch up what I'm doing right when she's about to come.

And right now, I'm sucking her clit into my mouth while teasing it with the tip of my tongue. It's driving her crazy. I can feel her arousal slipping over my lips and chin and down onto my throat. Such a fucking turn-on how wet she gets for me.

She pants the word "yes" over and over again as her pussy begins to flutter on my chin. She cries out, and her thighs squeeze hard around my face, and I can't catch a breath. But I don't care.

I don't need oxygen to survive.

All I need are her screams and this tight little pussy.

"Whew!" She laughs and crawls down my body to drape across me. Her chin rests on her hands on my chest. "I missed that mouth."

I lick my lips, getting every bit of her that I can. But I'm still a mess with it all over my chin and cheeks. I take a deep breath and look down at her.

"Did you also miss my cock? Because he's ready for round two if you want to untie me."

"Why would I have to untie you to use your cock?" Her eyebrow arches playfully.

"Because I can fuck you like you need to be fucked if I have full range of motion," I tease her back.

She lifts herself up and kisses me, tasting herself on my tongue as it sweeps into her mouth. I tug at the pillowcases that are keeping my hands tied to the headboard, but she did a damn good job of making sure I wouldn't be able to pull myself free. She laughs against my mouth as I continue to fight against them.

"It's not fair," I complain. "You've gotten to touch me all over. And I want to touch you."

"Yeah? What else do you want to do to me, baby?"

I lift my head to kiss her again and take the opportunity to bite her lip.

"I want to flip you over onto your back, throw those long-ass legs over my shoulders, and fuck you so deep while I hold that favorite wand of yours to your clit."

She hums and smiles with a little glint in her eyes.

"I want to fuck you until you see stars, Ivy. I want to fuck you until the only words you can say are 'yes' and 'more.'"

"And you need your hands for that?"

"Woman!"

She laughs and reaches up to start untying the knots. Once one is free, I reach over and untie the other one with urgency before wrapping my arms around her and flipping us over.

Ivy is in a fit of laughter at my eagerness and tugs me down to kiss her again. The kisses are sweet and slow, and my sensitive cock slides between us. She wraps her legs around me to pull me tighter against her body, upping the friction of her wet pussy on my cock.

"You're going to make me come before I'm even inside of you," I whisper against her mouth. I feel her lips curve into a smile.

"Well, we wouldn't want that. I'm not sure you could rally for round three."

"Excuse me?" I shout in mock outrage at the same time that she dissolves into another fit of laughter.

This woman.

"I'll have you know, boss lady, that I could rally for four if I really wanted to."

"Only if you *really* wanted to?"

"You have a smart mouth."

"You like it."

I lean back down and kiss her again before reaching over to grab the vibrator from the nightstand. She must've gotten it out of her suitcase when she got the crop. I wish we had more to play with, but that'll come later. If she really wants to keep this up, we have all the time and the toys in the world.

"Yes, I do." I move my hips so that the head of my cock lines up with her pussy as my mouth moves to kiss and nibble at her neck. I can still smell her shampoo when I breathe her in. "I like everything about you, actually."

I push just the tip inside of her, savoring the feel of her. She runs her hands up my chest and over my shoulders. Her nails dig into the skin of my arms. I sink another couple of inches inside of her and get quite the ego boost when her mouth drops open and her eyes roll a bit.

"God, you feel so good," she says in that breathy voice of hers. "I love the way you fuck me."

Thrusting the rest of the way in, I hold myself still while she adjusts before moving my arms and her legs so that they're held up by my shoulders. She's flexible, so she easily bends in half. The new position brings us even closer together and my cock even deeper inside of her. I click on the wand to a steady buzz and shuffle it between us. One hand holds on to it, keeping it in place, while the other makes sure I don't crush her under my weight.

Her pussy immediately clamps down on my cock, her clit so sensitive she can barely handle it. A low groan makes its way through her chest and out of her pretty mouth. I have to take a second to close my eyes and breathe. This feels too fucking good, and I want it to last.

"Do not hold back," she demands through gritted teeth. "I want it rough. I want to feel you between my legs tomorrow when I'm sitting on the airplane. I want to feel you when I get home and only have my vibrator to take the edge off."

"Fuck," I groan before I slowly pull out of her and then thrust back in. "Hold on."

14

Holding the vibrator against her clit and fucking her with all my strength is an accomplishment I should be allowed to put on my resume. The amount of balance and coordination this takes is worth some praise.

And goddamn does she give it to me.

"Oh, fuck, Greg. Do you know how good you feel inside of me, baby?" she asks as I plow into her as roughly as I can manage. "Your cock fills up my little pussy, stretching it to its limit. God, you feel so fucking good. Fuck me so good, baby."

She's so wet the noises we're making are louder than the vibrator. My hips piston, and her face contorts as her orgasm builds. I know she's sensitive by now, having had a few orgasms already tonight. And I'm hoping that the combination of that, this vibrator, and my cock will make her squirt. I fucking love it when she squirts all over me, making a mess for me to clean up after.

"Greg," she says on a moan. "Do not stop."

One of her hands moves between us to take the wand and

hold it exactly where she needs it. With her taking control of that, I'm able to get better leverage, holding myself up with both arms on the headboard to angle just right.

My ass and thighs are burning with the effort I'm putting in. Beads of sweat roll down my chest and abs, and my hair falls in my face. My lungs are on fucking fire, but with a few more pumps, Ivy is squeezing me.

Her pussy clamps around my cock, sucking me in as she comes and squirts. Her whole body flushes with pleasure, and I move so that her legs can drop from my shoulders. They're trembling, and I sit back on my heels to massage the muscles. I take the wand from her and turn it off, tossing it to the side so that she can recoup.

"Hey," I say softly, getting her to open her eyes and look at me. For a second, I was worried she had passed out on me.

"Sorry." She exhales and opens her eyes, blinking around to look at me. "That was intense. Like, really intense."

I continue to massage her, ignoring the need for my own release to make sure she's still okay and ready to continue. She takes some deep breaths, and her legs stop shaking. I'm still inside of her, and I can feel when the aftershocks of her orgasm finally settle down.

"You made a mess," I tease her. "I can't wait to clean you up after."

She smiles up at me and then pulls herself up to flip us over. Fuck yes, she's going to ride me until I come. This is what I wanted. She hovers over me, propped up on wobbly knees, and slowly sinks back down onto my dick.

The sensation is strange after having your cock beaten with a crop. I'm sore, and yet the soft muscles inside of her massage me so fucking good. But I know tomorrow —well, I guess today— I'm going to really be feeling this shit. My poor dick is going to be sore for a few days.

"Fuck, you ride me so good. Look at you."

Her tits bounce up and down with the timing of her hips. She knows exactly how I like it. She knows I like to watch. I've never been the guy who likes my women super thin. Not that there's anything wrong with being a size two; everyone just has their own preferences.

And mine is women like Ivy. I like the way her stretch marks stripe vertically across her belly and hips. There's a little horizontal line right at her belly button from the crease in her tummy rolls. And I love her heavy, full breasts that are far more than a handful. Even the curve of what she insists is a triple chin is beautiful to me.

Everything about her is soft and easy to grab onto. Her skin is smooth, and her thighs are strong. Fuck, this woman makes me crazy. Maybe I don't like *all* women like this. Maybe I just like Ivy.

"You're gorgeous, Ivy."

That brazen confidence she carries all the time softens a little with my words. She's a confident woman, and she loves her body and everything about it. But that doesn't mean she doesn't need to hear that she's beautiful. Everyone needs to hear that shit.

She leans forward and wraps her hand around my throat, squeezing the sides and smirking down at me.

"This gorgeous woman wants you to come."

"Yeah?" I taunt her, grabbing onto her hips until her flesh turns red. "You need me to fill you up, Ivy? Need me to fill up this tight little pussy?"

She nods and then leans down further to kiss me. It gives me a better angle to fuck her from underneath, and I go to fucking town. With her permission to come, I can chase my own orgasm and let go.

I close my eyes and give over to the sensation of her hand

around my throat and her cunt around my cock. It doesn't take long for the heat to spread through my entire body, making my muscles tense and my balls tighten.

"That's it, baby," she murmurs in my ear. "Let go. Come for me."

One last thrust and I come, emptying myself inside of her. I hold our bodies together as my toes curl. When I open my eyes to look up at her, she's smiling and watching me, waiting for me to finish so that she can relax and kiss me.

My cock slips free of her, and she curls against my body like a koala, holding on to me like she's afraid I'll disappear. With the last bit of energy I have, I wrap my arms around her and kiss the top of her head.

I'm so tired, and it's so late. I have no idea what time it is, but it has to be close to sunrise. We both have to be out of here by eleven, and I have a flight to catch just after one. Before falling asleep, I vaguely wonder if she has a wake-up call coming because if not, the maids might get a little bit more than they bargained for when they come in to clean.

15

Ivy groans and rolls away from me, jolting me out of the deepest sleep I think I've ever been in.

"What time is it?" I ask, my mouth dry and my head fucking pounding. I'm never drinking again.

I hear her shuffle stuff around on the nightstand, and then she emits another groan.

"Seven. We've been asleep for all of maybe three hours. If that."

"I feel like I've been hit by a train. Please tell me you also feel like you've been hit by a train?"

She laughs at me, and then the warmth of her body comes back to me.

"I also feel like I've been hit by a train, yes. That's what happens when you drink shot after shot of moonshine and then stay up all night having sex." She kisses my chest and then heaves her legs on top of mine, tangling our limbs together.

We haven't showered, and I feel gross. I also feel like I

wasted an opportunity falling asleep before I could clean my girl up. Now we're just lying here in each other's cum and sweat.

Yummy.

I kiss her forehead. "Let's shower."

"Let's not move a muscle," she volleys back.

I laugh. "Ivy, we have to be out of here in a few hours, and we're covered in bar smells, cum, and sweat."

She doesn't open her eyes, but she sticks her bottom lip out in a pout and makes a little *huff* through her nose.

"I know you're right." She hugs me tighter but still doesn't open her eyes. "But the second we get out of bed, this special little one-night bubble we're in gets popped."

"It's not that we're going to leave this bed and never see each other again. What happened to you retiring? What happened to us dating and trying this out for real?" I poke her in her side. "Getting cold feet already, boss lady?"

She laughs and finally opens those pretty blue eyes to look at me.

"I wasn't sure if that was the liquor talking."

"For you or for me?" I ask. "Because if you retiring was the liquor talking, I fully support the liquor."

"For you!" she says through her laughter. "It was a lot to throw on someone."

"No, it wasn't. You were just *asking me out*, Ivy. People do that every day."

She shrugs.

"The only reason I thought we ended this was because we were breaking all the rules. We were sneaking around, hoping no one would catch us. It would've reflected horribly on both of us." I push the hair out of her face and smile over at her. "But if you retire, that means we won't have that hanging over our heads. We'll just be a normal couple."

"With a massive age gap." She gives me a look, and I can't help but snort in her face.

"I'd hardly call fifteen years *massive*." I roll my eyes.

"Not embarrassed to be seen in public all the time with a woman that much older than you?"

"Ivy...no. What? No. One, have you seen yourself? No one is ever going to guess you're older than me. Two, it doesn't matter what other people think because they aren't us—they don't get a say about our relationship."

"Ooh," she teases, tickling my sides. "Our relationship."

"Don't deflect," I chide her, playfully pushing away her wild hands. "If you really want to do this, I will do this. After I get back to California from this next work trip, let me take you out."

"I'm giving notice next week, but I won't leave until the end of the quarter. I wanted to see them through Q4."

"So, you don't want to go out until the new year?" I ask, a little put off about the fact she *still* doesn't want to be seen with me, even with everyone knowing she's retiring. Especially since it would be a long shot for someone to see us out in public anyway. We live in a big-ass city. It's hard to run into people.

"No, no, that's not what I meant." Her smile is soft, and it melts my heart a little. She's looking at me like I mean something to her, and that's new. I like it. "I was just letting you know the plan. I am more than happy to try this the moment you get back. Toronto, I'm guessing, is where you're off to next?"

"Ugh," I groan. "Yeah."

"It'll fly by. I know it's a long week of training, but those things always end up going faster than you think."

"Okay, enough shop talk. Can we please shower now?

Now that you've been reassured that this is not the last time you'll ever get to experience my magic dick?"

She bursts out laughing.

"You are so full of yourself. When did I say I didn't want to leave this bed because of your dick?"

"My mouth, then?"

She giggles.

"My fingers?"

"Oh, my god. Shut up," she groans through her laughter, but I soldier on.

"I know it's not because of my morning breath."

"Okay, okay! I'm up!" She rolls out of bed and tugs the covers off me as some sick and twisted form of punishment.

My poor, bruised cock is on display.

"Up!" she says, smacking my leg playfully. "And maybe we can take care of *that* in the shower?" Ivy points at my hardening dick and then struts away, her peachy ass swaying with each step.

I scramble to get out of bed, tripping and falling out instead because I'm in such a rush. She didn't see what happened, but she definitely heard it because a snort comes from the adjoining bathroom before the rush of water.

When I finally manage to get off the floor and into the bathroom, she's brushing her long hair in the mirror. I take the brush from her and do it myself. My love language is definitely acts of service like this because I love the way I'm able to take something off her plate. Anything I can do is one less thing she has to worry about.

"You dyed your hair," I point out. "I forgot to tell you. I like it."

She smiles at me in the mirror. "I found a grey hair, and I think it drove me a little crazy. This feels a little bit too dark, but I was determined to cover it up."

"I think it looks good." I finish with her hair as the steam starts to fog up the mirror and then kiss her cheek. "But I would also think you looked good if your whole head was grey."

She rolls her eyes and playfully shoves me out of the way.

"Shut up."

"No, I'm serious," I say, following her into the shower. "I could tell everyone I was fucking a silver fox!"

"Gregory!" she scolds me through her laughter. "Never say that again."

I just shrug.

"Just sayin'." I wink at her when she looks over her shoulder. "It's hot, baby."

16

"Think we have time to squeeze in one more orgasm?" I ask her once we're both inside. The water is too hot for me, but I know she likes to shower in hellfire, so I just grit my teeth and bear it, hoping my skin won't melt off in the twenty minutes we're in here.

"Me or you?" Her mouth slants into a smirk.

"Well, I was hoping both."

She hums and steps fully back into the water. There's steam billowing up around us as she wets her hair. It looks like an oil slick with that new black hair of hers, and I can't help but reach out and run my hands through it.

"Let me wash your hair?"

"Oh my god, yes, please."

She finishes wetting it thoroughly and then turns around, leaning her head back so that I can wash it for her. Women love this shit, and I love doing it for her. She brought her fruity-scented shampoo, and I lather a liberal amount into her hair. I press the tips of my fingers into her scalp and massage away all of her stress.

Leaning her body back into me, she sighs and moans as my fingers move down to her neck and shoulders. She melts into me, and I let her use my body to prop up her own as I reach for the detachable showerhead and begin to rinse. How her scalp doesn't melt off, I don't know.

"God, that feels fantastic."

I kiss her wet hair. "I'm glad you think so. I'm pretty sure I'm melting."

"You're such a wimp," she laughs. "Always taking your tepid showers. The heat relaxes the muscles."

"Or tenses them if you're in pain from the scalding."

I hook the showerhead back to the faucet, and she turns around to face me, rolling her eyes.

"Hand me the conditioner?"

She nods toward the bottle behind me. I hand it to her, and she works it into the ends of her hair. After she's done working her hair up into a bun and held back with a claw clip, she picks up the soap and hands it to me.

"My body next?"

I grin and then spin her around, pulling her back to my front before getting some bodywash and then putting the bottle to the side. Her skin is soft and smooth, and when I run my hands over her breasts, her nipples are pebbled from the heat of the water. Her skin is a pretty pink color under the suds of the soap.

I make sure to lather up every square inch of her body, touching her and teasing her. I dip between her thighs, just a little, just to taunt her. She groans and lays her head back on my shoulder, grabbing my hand and forcing it back down her body.

The water streams down over both of us, letting all the

soap suds rinse down the drain. I let her guide me to where she wants me. She lifts one of her legs up on the small seat that's in the shower, giving me the best access to her pussy.

When I part her open and slip a finger inside, she rewards me by moaning my name. My name has never sounded so sweet. I bring her wetness up to her clit, circling it with the tip of my finger just as she reaches behind her to grab onto my dick.

Her hand twists slightly as she strokes me, squeezing when she gets to the head. Fuck, that feels amazing. She even takes a moment each time to run the tips of her fingers on that sensitive spot underneath. I can't even think about the soreness from last night. Her hand and the warm water are making that nonexistent.

"I want to come like this," she says, looking up at me over her shoulder. "Together. I want us to come at the same time."

"Okay, boss lady," I agree with a smirk. "We can do that."

I lean forward and kiss her, but the position we're in makes it a little difficult to do it for very long. So instead, she just lays her head back on my shoulder, and we watch each other.

Extended eye contact used to freak me out—it felt too personal and too deep. But looking into her eyes right now as we both chase our pleasure, I'm surprised at how much I love it. Her eyes hold me captive, and my heart rate kicks out of control.

I dip two fingers inside of her and watch as her mouth drops open on a gasp. Her hand pumps me faster, the rhythm in time with my fingers inside of her. I dip inside and then swirl her clit, over and over. Our chests move at the same time, heaving as the heat spreads through both of our bodies. And the entire time, our eyes stay locked on one another.

"I'm going to come," she whines. "Tell me you're close. I can't hold back."

"I'm close, baby," I whisper. "Keep going. Just like that. It feels so fucking good."

Her free hand goes to her nipples, pulling and twisting them as her orgasm builds. I can feel my own—I'm right on the edge. Just a few...more...strokes.

"I'm coming!" I cry out just as her pussy clamps down around my fingers.

I shoot all over her ass as her fist slows, and my fingers halt their movements inside of her. Her eyes flutter, and she looks so fucking beautiful. I push her hand away and pull out of her to spin her around to face me. Grabbing onto her face, I pull her to me in a bruising kiss.

This I could get used to. Waking up every day to her in bed and playing in the shower together. Then having her again when I come home in the evenings. I'll get to show her off in public—finally. And we can live our lives the way we should've been able to the first time we tried this.

She can finally be *mine*.

"Mine," I growl into her mouth when I can't hold back the feelings anymore.

She looks up at me with dazed eyes.

"Huh?" she asks like she didn't hear me. But she did. She just wants to hear it again.

"Mine." I nip at her bottom lip. "You're mine. And I'm yours, Ivy. Everyone will know it. It's how it should've been the first time we got together."

"But we couldn't—"

"I know we couldn't." One of my hands leaves her hair to grab hold of her round ass. "But we can now. And I'm not letting you go again. I want this every day. All of this. You.

The late-night junk food. The sex. All the shitty dancing you drag me to."

She laughs. "Yeah?"

"I want the dating, hopefully the marriage, maybe the kids. Whatever you want, I'm down for. I want to give you the life you said you've missed out on the two decades. Anything you want, Ivy. I will give it to you."

Her eyes tear up as she looks up at me.

"You're sure? You want all of that with a forty-five-year-old woman? I'll understand if you don't, Gregory. It's a lot to ask. It's a lot all at once, I—"

I shut her up with a kiss.

"Shut up, boss lady."

She snorts and wipes at her eyes.

"You want all of it," she repeats.

I smile and nod.

"All of it."

And I seal the promise with a kiss.

17

I pulled one of the chairs in the room closer to the bathroom so that I could sit and talk to her while she got ready. I've been watching her curl her hair with this new brush thing that also doubles as a hair dryer. After each strand she dries and curls, she wraps it around a pink roller and pins it to her head. By the time she's done, her head is covered in big black and pink blobs that make her four inches taller.

Her makeup is artistry. That's the only way I can explain it. She's beautiful without it, and with it, she's equally as stunning. She takes the time to blend everything out, curl her lashes, and make a sharp point with her eyeliner. She meets my gaze in the mirror before she starts taking out her curlers.

"You're staring."

"You're gorgeous."

She rolls her eyes.

"You're a flatterer."

"You're stunning."

"Gregory." She gives me a look in the mirror, but I can see the blush come through her cheeks.

She pulls the rollers out one by one, fluffing the chunks of hair with her fingers as she goes. Once they're all out, she takes a brush through them, and they soften but still lie over her shoulders in pretty waves.

"I was thinking," I say to get her attention. "Come with me to Toronto."

She turns around, leans back against the bathroom counter, and crosses her arms under her chest. It's very distracting as it pushes her tits up. She's already in a sexy black set that has been way too hard to keep my hands off.

"You want me to come to the training week with you?" Her eyebrows are pulled together. "Why?"

"Because I miss you. And I don't want to say goodbye to you for a week after I just got you back." I shrug. "Take a week off. Come with me. Turn in your intent to retire after. One week won't make a big deal in the grand scheme of things."

"Won't you be too busy? Those training weeks are hellish. You'll need to rest."

"I'd rather rest with you."

"Gregory..."

"Do I need to beg?" I smirk over at her. "I'll get out of this chair and crawl over to you, begging on my hands and knees."

"That's an overreaction, don't you think?" She bites back a smile.

"Anything for you," I tell her as I scoot out of the chair and fall to my hands and knees.

"Gregory!" she laughs. "Knock it off."

I crawl a few paces toward her, smiling up at her while she just laughs and watches me.

"We do not have time for this! No more playtime!"

She cackles as I reach her and grab onto her ankles, crawling up her body until my hands are grabbing handfuls of her ass and my mouth is kissing her stomach.

"Please come to Toronto with me, Ivy," I beg her, my face all smiles as she laughs down at me. God, I want to make this woman laugh for the rest of our lives.

"Okay, fine!" she concedes, and I stand up, pulling her into my arms and spinning her around in a circle. It's like I've won the lottery, and all I've done is convinced her to tag along on this stupid training week.

"You're too good to me." I stand and kiss her hard on the mouth, careful not to mess up her makeup.

"I still have to go home first," she tells me as I plop back into the chair.

"Go home. Pack enough for a week, and then fly up. My flight is at one today, but I think I can survive a day without you." I wink at her, and I'm rewarded with another eye roll.

"Careful," I warn her. "Roll your eyes too much and they'll roll right out of your head."

"That is the daddest of dad jokes I think I've ever heard you say." She gives me a playful shove and walks past me back into the bedroom. "I'll fly out tomorrow *after* I hand in my intent."

"Why after?"

"Because if I'm coming with you to a company event, I don't want it hanging over our heads when we stay in the same room or go out to eat." She throws on some leggings that hug her ass, and when she turns around, she catches me staring. "Did you hear a word I said?"

"Yep." I nod, having the decency to look perfectly chastised. "Handing in your notice so that we don't feel like we have rules when you come up to Toronto. Got it."

She shakes her head and smiles. "Good boy. You've always been decent at multitasking."

"Decent?" I act insulted. "I'm a fantastic multitasker, thank you. Pretty sure I was multitasking perfectly well last night when I held the vibrator to your clit while also fucking the shit out of you."

When her head pops through the top of her sweater, her mouth drops open.

"God, you've got a mouth on you."

"You love my mouth," I say, standing and walking over to her.

She runs her fingers over my lips. "Yes, I do." She leans forward and gives me a quick peck. "Now, go get your shit from your room. I'll meet you downstairs, and I can take you to the airport."

I check my watch. It's nearly eleven, and I'm still in my clothes from last night. It would be nice to put clean clothes on since I showered. So I leave her for now and run down to my room to get everything together.

After everything is packed up and I've changed into a fresh set of clothes, I take a second to go through my phone. I have a few work emails to respond to and a couple of text messages from the group. Opening up the thread, I scroll back to the top of what I missed.

First, there's a picture of Hudson holding Lucy with a big-ass bow on her head and a toothless smile. He's dressed to match her outfit. That man is obsessed with that baby girl. It makes me happy to think he finally got his happily ever after.

WES

> Think we haven't heard from Greg because he's fucking his boss?

QUIN

> *eye roll emoji* You're an ass. Leave him alone! If he wants to fuck his boss he can.

ZOË

> I slapped him for that comment.

QUIN

> Good.

I type up a response.

ME

> In fact, yeah. I was fucking my boss. I actually was last year when we were in Tokyo, and for a couple months after that. But then we stopped. Because, ya know, rules and decorum and all that shit. But she's retiring, so we're giving this another go. Like an honest to god go of it. I like her. Be nice.

    I toss my phone to the side and do one last sweep, making sure I've got everything before I zip everything up and check my phone again. There's a flood of new messages congratulating me and apologizing for taking the piss. After shooting off another message telling them thanks and that I'll talk to them more later, I shove my phone in my pocket and head out the door.

    I never thought that this stupid little weekend business trip would lead to this. Honestly, I thought we were done after we broke things off last year. I think we both thought the other was less attached than ourselves, but I am fucking stoked to find out that that was never the case.

    Ivy likes me. She wants to date me, be with me, show me

off. No more keeping what we are to each other in secret. That woman is mine, and I'm hers.

Fuck, this is a good feeling.

EPILOGUE

When I travel, I don't really care about where I'm staying. A king bed and a room with a relatively nice view is all I care about. But once I asked Ivy to tag along with me on this trip, I knew I needed to upgrade to something different. It's not that she's high-maintenance—okay, maybe she is. But she wouldn't have an issue staying in whatever room I got; I just want to let this be a nice trip for her.

So I canceled my reservation and booked a penthouse in the city. It's going to add about twenty to thirty minutes to my commute for the training seminars, but I don't really care. This is going to make Ivy happy. That's what I care about.

She flew home from Nashville, and I flew here two days ago. And now I'm just waiting at the airport with a sign that I know is going to make her smile and blush at the same time.

"Mistress Ivy" is written in bold, bright red letters on this white piece of paper I hold at my chest. I get a lot of side-eye as people walk past me, but when she finally walks through the gate into baggage claim, the way her face lights up with embarrassment is so worth it.

"Gregory!" she whisper yells. "Are you kidding me?" She takes the paper from my hands and crumples it up as we come together for a kiss. In public. God, this feels too fucking good.

"What?" I act stupid with an innocent smile. "I thought you'd like it."

"You're such a brat." She groans and acts annoyed, but I can tell she secretly loves it. My girl likes to be doted on. And in public. In. Fucking. Public.

Finally.

After we get her bags, we head into the city to the penthouse I've rented out for the week. I was in training meetings all day, so I'm ready to go out with her for food and drinks and then bring her back and fuck her into oblivion.

It's only been a couple of days, but I've been craving this woman like an addict. I can't get enough. I've rubbed one out too many times to count since the last time I saw her. And sitting in the car with her isn't helping. Her scent wraps around like a fucking vise grip, making my cock rock hard in my pants.

I have a feeling dinner is going to be the last thing on either of our minds once we're alone.

And goddamn, was I right. The second we're inside and I put her bags on the floor, she pushes me up against the door, slamming it shut in the process. She's on me like a heat-seeking missile. Her mouth kisses me, her hands pull my shirt up so that she can feel the muscles underneath, and her hips push into my own.

After I get over the initial shock, I grab onto her ass and pull her as close as she possibly can be. And then the frantic undressing starts. She pulls off my shirt, and I unbutton her jeans. She starts on my pants while I tug her shirt over her head. Something rips in the process, but we're too lost in what we're doing to know whose it was or even care.

She pushes my pants and boxers down over my hips, and gravity does the rest of the work. My cock bobs free between us, the precum on the tip rubbing against her stomach as we kiss like we're each other's oxygen.

Dropping to my knees, I pull her jeans all the way down, leaving the silky panties on. I love the way she looks in lingerie, and I've decided I want to fuck her with it on. There's a dark spot from how wet she is, and when I cover it with my mouth, she moans and leans forward, propping herself up on the door.

Her hair falls forward, touching the top of my head, and her eyes close as the heat of my mouth teases her slit. Her other hand goes to my hair, ruffling the soft strands as I flatten my tongue against her.

"Fuck me against this door." Her voice is breathy and full of arousal.

"I'd prefer to take my time with you," I say, smirking up at her. I know she's going to get her way. After all, she is in charge. But I can't help but fight back a little. I wouldn't be me if I didn't.

"I've been missing you for days." She moans when I move her panties and slip a finger into her wetness. "We can take our time later, baby. Just fuck me."

"How attached are you to these?" I ask, gesturing to the panties I'm currently holding to the side as I play.

"I don't—" Her voice stutters when I circle her clit. "I don't care. Why do you care?"

"Because I want to fuck you in this gorgeous set," I tell her as I take ahold of the fabric. "But if I'm fucking you against this door, they're going to be in the way."

With a harsh pull, I rip the fabric apart, right over her center. She gasps, but I'm already standing up and covering her mouth with mine. I spin us around and grab her ass, lifting her off the floor and pressing her back against the cool wood of the door. Her nails dig into my shoulders as I line myself up. She's so fucking wet that I'm able to slide right in, filling her to the hilt.

"Oh, fuck." Her head drops forward, and our foreheads touch as I begin to thrust inside of her.

The silky bra she's wearing can barely contain her breasts. They spill over the edge as they bounce in time with my hips. The door creaks, and her legs tighten their grip around my waist.

"I'm not gonna last long," I tell her, half laughing when I feel the orgasm already building. "Please tell me you're close."

"I am," she pants. "I am. Just keep hitting that spot."

"Play with yourself. I want to watch."

Her hand darts between us, pushing the strip of fabric out of the way so that she can tease her clit. Her fingers circle and scissor around it, and her moans get louder. With every few strokes, she'll let them dip further down and squeeze my cock before going back to her clit.

The extra sensation each time she does that makes my balls tighten. It feels so fucking good being inside of her, her tight cunt sucking me in and massaging my cock with every thrust.

"I'm going to come," she says, opening her eyes and staring into mine.

"Thank god," I groan, and she laughs.

My glutes are on fire, but I don't stop. The heat builds in my spine and explodes just as she cries out her own release.

We kiss, and I bite her lower lip, moaning as her walls pulse around me, heightening every bit of pleasure I get.

Our bodies are sweaty from the exertion, and our skin sticks together when she collapses into me, resting her head on my shoulder.

"God, I needed that," she admits. "I think my poor vibrator has been worn out in the last couple days."

I laugh and kiss her hair. "My forearm has bulked up a bit since the last time I saw you, too. I'm a man possessed."

We catch our breath, and she kisses me softly.

"How about we order in?" she asks. "I don't think I want to leave this place or your bed all night."

At the prospect of getting to fuck her again, my cock starts to harden inside of her. The little guy is rallying already. I'm impressed.

"Already?" she asks, her eyes widening.

"What can I say? Silver foxes just do it for me."

I swallow her laughter with a kiss and carry her off to bed.

EXTENDED EPILOGUE

Almost a year later...

"Where is the birthday girl?" I shout as we walk into the birthday party.

"Shh!" Ivy chastises as she walks in behind me. "What if she's napping?"

"At her birthday party?" I ask, raising an eyebrow in her direction.

"You never know. Babies sleep whenever and wherever they want."

"Through here!" I hear Hudson call from the direction of the kitchen.

"See," I tell her, readjusting the presents under my arms. "Everyone else is yelling."

"Thought we'd be the last to get here," I tell them as we walk in. "Hit mad traffic on the way here. It was insane."

"Wes called a few minutes ago," Quinlan says from

where she's chopping veggies at the counter. "They must've hit the same traffic you did. But they'll be here soon."

Aurora walks in, Lucy on her hip.

"Look how big you are!" I coo at her. I place all the presents on the kitchen island and walk over to her. She reaches out for me, and I eagerly take her from Aurora.

Babies *love* me.

She mumbles and grabs onto my shirt as I dance around the room with her. Ivy watches me from the seat she's taken up next to Owen. We've talked about kids. I know she really wants them, and I'm not opposed to it. But it's only been a year, and I don't want to make this decision too quickly.

I still have to travel a lot for work, and even though she says she wouldn't mind staying home with our kid while I'm gone, I hate the thought of leaving all of that on her. If we're going to do this, I want to do it right. I want to find a job that lets me be home more—lets me help more.

"Okay, my turn!" Quinlan says, wiping her hands on her jeans and smiling as she walks over to take Lucy. This kid loves us all and happily transfers people. I don't think she has been put down a moment in her life. Spoiled little thing.

Grabbing a beer from the fridge, I go stand next to Jack, who is watching Quin with sad eyes. I can't even imagine the shit they're going through right now if they're still trying. Especially when they're always around Lucy.

"How's things going on your end?" I ask him, pulling his attention from Quin.

He sighs. "It's alright, man."

"Still trying?" I ask, nodding toward where Quinlan now dances in circles while Lucy giggles.

"Yeah." He laughs humorlessly. "Fruitlessly, clearly. We've talked about IVF all year, but I don't want to put her body through that, and I don't think she wants to either.

We've been to doctors, gotten our counts tested, and no one can really tell us why it isn't happening. It just...isn't."

I put my hand on his shoulder and give it a squeeze.

"I'm so sorry, Jack. I can't imagine."

I take a drink of my beer, and he just nods, his stare going back to Quin.

"Can I ask? Have y'all thought about adopting?"

He glances over at me, his eyes a bit happier.

"We have, actually." He sits his drink down and turns to face me. "Don't tell anyone. We aren't ready yet. But we've started the paperwork."

"Holy shit, dude. That's amazing!" I try to keep my voice down, but damn, I'm so happy for them. They've been trying for almost two years now. "You'll make the best parents. Any kid would be lucky to have you guys."

"Thanks, man. We're hopeful but trying not to get our hopes too high in the sky, ya know? This shit is tough. Lots of hoops to jump through."

"The party has arrived!" I hear Wes scream from the entryway.

"Wesley!" Zoë chides. "What if Lucy is sleeping!"

I meet Ivy's eyes, and she gives me a look that says, *I told you so*.

"She's not! You're fine!" Owen calls out to them as they follow our voices to the kitchen.

"Still," Zoë says when she walks in. "He could try to have some sense about him."

She walks around to the girls, saying hello and giving them hugs. They all walk outside together because Aurora wants to show them the garden they had someone come to put in a couple of weeks ago.

"So," Wes says, clapping his hands together. "Who wants the news?"

"Oh, Christ. Did you knock that poor girl up?" Hudson groans.

"Pyro, not everyone in this friend group is trying to have babies." Wes rolls his eyes. "No. We are not pregnant."

He looks around and then holds his left hand up in the air. It takes a second, but then I see it. The thick black band around his ring finger.

"You're married?" I shout, my excitement not letting me use my inside voice.

"*Yes we are!*" he bellows so loudly I think the glassware in the kitchen cabinets rattles.

"Wesley!" Zoë yells, her footsteps stomping back into the house. "You promised we would tell them together!"

"Sorry, babe." He smiles and shrugs. And I think for a moment she's really going to let him have it in front of all of us, but before she can, the girls come running, asking to see the ring. And she's quickly pulled back outside in a fit of laughter and squeals over the ring.

"Congratulations, Wes," Owen says, pulling him in for a hug. Hudson follows, and then Jack and I join in. It becomes quite the sappy hugfest between all five of us for a moment.

"Since when?" Pyro asks.

"About a week ago," he tells us. His face is lit up with happiness.

"Look at all of us," Jack says, handing Wes a beer. "All paired up. All happy. Can you imagine what our younger selves would say?"

"Mine would be shocked I was in a throuple," Owen deadpans, making us all burst out laughing.

"Mine would be thrilled," Hudson adds, wagging his eyebrows at Owen as he pulls him in for a kiss. Owen's face turns a bright shade of pink, but damn does he look happy as shit.

"Mine would be shocked I was thinking about marrying my boss," I say.

"Ex-boss," Wes points out.

"Fair," I agree.

"I think mine would be shocked I actually got someone to stay with me," Jack adds.

"I think we're all a bit shocked by that one, bro," Hudson says, laughing. "With those...tendencies you have."

Jack shoves him, making him almost topple over with Owen still wrapped in his arms. We all laugh for a second before going quiet, taking drinks from our beers and just kind of sitting with the moment.

It feels weird, all of us being here but no longer alone. All of us have those beautiful women outside. Our friend group has literally doubled, and it feels like we're moving into a different phase of our lives. One where we're still friends, and always will be, but where we all have someone else that comes first now.

"Fuck it," Jack says, downing the rest of his beer. "I told Greg, but...Quin and I have filled out the paperwork to adopt."

I smile as I watch everyone hug and congratulate him. And I'm glad he decided to tell everyone. He and Quin don't have to be alone in this.

"We're here for you," Wes says. "Literally, here. Because Zoë and I have decided to put down some roots. We're tired of traveling and being away from you guys all the time. We're moving home."

"Oh, fuck yes!" Pyro shouts. "Back together! Back together!" he chants, bouncing on his toes.

"Hey! A toast," Jack says, holding his bottle in the middle of our circle. "To the original five and the other four that saved us."

"Five," Owen corrects, winking at Jack. "Don't leave out your niece."

"To the five who saved us," he amends.

We all clink our bottles together and then take a swig.

"Who's ready to eat?" Aurora sings as all the girls come back inside.

"Me! Fucking starving!" Wes says, and I don't miss the glare Zoë throws his way.

"Quin is trying to adopt!" Ivy whispers when she comes over to me.

"Jack told us. How awesome is that?"

She pushes up on her tiptoes and kisses me.

"And Wes and Zoë are moving home," I tell her.

She gives me the sweetest smile.

I look around the kitchen, watching all of my friends with their partners laugh and joke, fighting over food and who gets to hold Lucy. We're so different than we were five years ago.

But I can't say I'm sorry about it.

"All back together again," she murmurs, stealing my attention back to her.

I smile back and kiss the tip of her nose.

"All back together again," I agree.

DANA'S OTHER WORKS

Read the rest of the One Night Series here:
https://amzn.to/3BmZ4h0

If you want to explore Dana's other works:
https://www.amazon.com/author/danaisaly

And she would love it if you joined her on her socials!

Instagram: @author.danaisaly

TikTok: @author.disaly and @author.danaisaly

Facebook group: https://bit.ly/DanasTribe

ACKNOWLEDGMENTS

I can't believe it's over! When this all started, I really thought I was only going to tell Jack's story. But then you all fell in love with his gaggle of friends — and so did I. Thank you for sticking around to find out how they all turned out.

Thank you to Abi who has made every single cover for this series, and formatted each one to bring to life the vibe of these guys. Thank you for taking my incredibly vague ideas and turning them into masterpieces.

Thank you to Sandra, my editor, for making my books the best they can be. Also, I appreciate how you just pencil me in a week *after* when I tell you I'll have it by. My procrastination brain really, really digs that.

Thank you to Amber, Julia, Heather, and Megan who pushes me to keep going when all I could think about were cowboys. Thank you to Dee, Cady, Tori, K Leigh, and Em for giving me constant laughs to get me through the days. And thank you to Christopher for cheering me on when all I've wanted to do is quit.

Thank you to my readers who have been there cheering me on every step of the way. I see each and every one of you, and

I couldn't be happier to have you. You guys are all my family, and I love how you support me every day!

Keep an eye out...something special for this group is coming soon!

ABOUT THE AUTHOR

Dana Isaly is a Romance author that has dipped her toes in dark, paranormal, and even romcom.

She was born in the Midwest, grew up in the South, went to university in England, and even spent a couple years in California. She is a lover of books, coffee, and rainy days.

She swears too much, loves dogs more than people, and believes that love is love is love.

You can find her on Instagram (@author.danaisaly), join her Facebook group (Dana's Tribe of Horny Humans), or follow her on TikTok (@author.disaly).

Manufactured by Amazon.ca
Bolton, ON

34064702R00079